Sir Clements Robert Markham

Ollanta : an ancient Ynca drama

Sir Clements Robert Markham

Ollanta : an ancient Ynca drama

ISBN/EAN: 9783337305673

Printed in Europe, USA, Canada, Australia, Japan

Cover: Foto ©Andreas Hilbeck / pixelio.de

More available books at **www.hansebooks.com**

OLLANTA.

AN ANCIENT YNCA DRAMA.

TRANSLATED FROM THE ORIGINAL QUICHUA.

BY

CLEMENTS R. MARKHAM, C.B.,

Corresponding Member of the University of Chile.

LONDON:

TRÜBNER & CO., 60 PATERNOSTER ROW.

1871.

INTRODUCTION.

The literature of the Yncas of Peru consisted of love-songs, elegies, allegoric hymns, and dramatic compositions. Unfortunately, most of these evidences of ancient civilisation have disappeared, or are still in manuscript. The earliest writers knew little or nothing of them. They were preserved as traditions in the families of the conquered and fallen Yncas, and were not communicated to the Spaniards; who, indeed, took little pains to seek for them.

Garcilasso Ynca de la Vega * was the only author, contemporary with the first conquerors, who had a correct knowledge of the language of the Yncas; and the only one, therefore, whose testimony has any real value. He tells us little, but that little is important. We learn from his pages that the *Amautas* or philosophers of the Ynca court composed dramas relating to the deeds of former sovereigns and heroes, which were performed by persons of rank.† They also composed poems and love-songs with alternate long and short verses, having the right number of syllables in each; and

---

* All the references to Garcilasso, in this introduction, are to my English translation, printed for the Hakluyt Society.

† See my translation, vol. i. p. 194.

Garcilasso describes them as resembling the Spanish compositions called *redondillas*.* They had many other metres for these songs, and for the elegies recited by their *Harahuicus* or *Trouvères*. The Ynca poets also treated of the secondary causes, by means of which God acts in the region of the air to cause lightning, rain, and snow. Blas Valera preserved some verses of this kind, which he calls *spondaics*, and which are certainly of undoubted antiquity.†

These verses, and four lines of a love-song in Garcilasso,‡ are the only fragments of ancient Ynca literature that were preserved in the writings of early Spanish authors. Garcilasso also mentions a class of songs called *haylli*, in which the deeds of valiant warriors, and the hopes and fears of lovers, were celebrated. The word *haylli*, or "triumph," was used as a refrain or chorus; and the songs were chanted by the people when engaged in ploughing, and other field labours. §

The means of preserving ancient songs and dramas were rude, but not altogether ineffectual. They consisted of oral transmission, the same means by which, as Max Müller believes, the whole Vedic literature was preserved for centuries; and the system of *quipus* or knots. In his own account of the *quipus*, Garcilasso nowhere says that songs and traditions were preserved by their means alone. He merely states that the *Amautas* put the narratives of the

---

* Eight syllable lines broken into stanzas of four lines, and thence called *redondillas* or *roundelays*. See *Ticknor*, i. p. 102.

† *G. de la Vega*, i. p. 197. See also my Quichua Grammar and Dictionary (Trübner, 1864), p. 10.

‡ *Ibid.*   § *Ibid.* ii. p. 8.

historical events into the form of brief and easily remembered sentences, while the *Harahuicus** condensed them into pithy verses, both forms being prepared with a view to their being learnt by heart, and handed down by the people. But the *Quipu-camayocs,* or "keepers of knots," appear to have combined the duties of preserving and deciphering the knot records, with those of remembering and transmitting the historical narratives and songs; and Garcilasso implies that their memories, in some way which he does not explain, were assisted by the knots. "Each thread and knot," he says, "brought to the mind that which it was arranged it should suggest; just as the commandments and articles of our holy Catholic faith are remembered by the numbers under which they are placed." In giving the verses preserved by Blas Valera, however, the Ynca quotes from that writer, who says that he found the verses in knots of different colours, which recorded certain ancient annals.†

Such is all that is to be gathered from the writers who flourished in the century which witnessed the conquest of the Ynca empire by the Spaniards. We come next to the inquiry whether songs and dramatic compositions of præ-Spanish times were likely to be preserved, orally or in writing, by the Ynca chiefs and people. It was the policy of the Spaniards to treat the native chiefs with some consideration; they were allowed to retain the ancient insignia of their rank, and to appear in them in public religious processions,‡ and

---

* *G. de la Vega,* ii. p. 125.   † *Ibid.* i. p. 196.

‡ They are so represented in the pictures in the church of Santa Ana, at Cuzco.

they were placed in authority over their vassals as agents of the Spanish Corregidores.* They wore their peculiar dresses down to the time of the rebellion of Tupac Amaru † in 1780, after which their use was prohibited. It is thus clear that the Ynca chiefs were permitted by the Spaniards to retain a portion of their authority, that they were encouraged to continue the use of their costumes in order to increase the magnificence of religious processions, and that some at least of the old Ynca customs were preserved by special enactments. Under these favourable circumstances, the chiefs would almost certainly preserve the memory of the former grandeur of their country, and encourage the people to recite the ancient songs and dramas, some of which would

* "*Ordenanzas del Peru, por Don Francisco de Toledo, recogidas por el Lic. Don Tomas de Ballesteros*" (Lima, 1685).

Titulo VI. "*De los Caciques Principales.*" By *Ordenanza* xix. the Caciques and principal people were ordered to dine in the *plazas* of the villages where their vassals were accustomed to assemble, because it was considered right that, in this, the ancient customs of the Yncas should be preserved, and that the chiefs should eat publicly with the poor Indians. By other *Ordenanzas*, in the same *Titulo*, the native chiefs were charged with the superintendence of the morals of the people, of the repair of *andenes* (terraces) and *tambos* (rest-houses on the roads), and with other similar duties.

† In the sentence of death on Tupac Amaru, pronounced by the Visitador Areche at Cuzco, on May 15th, 1781, all dresses used by the Yncas and chiefs were thenceforth prohibited, including the *uncu* or mantle, and the *mascapaicha* or head-dress. All documents relating to the descent of the Yncas were ordered to be burnt, the representation of Quichua dramas was prohibited, all pictures of the Yncas were to be destroyed as well as musical instruments, and the Indians were ordered to give up their national dress, and to clothe themselves in the Spanish fashion.— *MS. penes C. R. M.* Also printed in Angelis.

eventually be committed to writing. The dramatic aptitude of the people was discovered by the Spanish priests almost immediately after the conquest, and they endeavoured, with notable success, to turn this talent to account, as a means of conveying religious instruction. Garcilasso tells us that the Jesuits composed dramas for the Indians to act, because they knew that this was the custom in the time of the Yncas, and because they saw that the Indians were so ready to receive instruction through that means. He adds that one of the Jesuits in a village near the shores of lake Titicaca, called Juli, composed a play in the dialect spoken in that part of the country,* on the enmity between the serpent and the seed of the woman, which was acted by Indian lads. Other plays on religious subjects were acted in the Quichua language at Potosi, Cuzco, and Lima; and Garcilasso assures us that the lads repeated the dialogues with so much grace, feeling, and correct action, that they gave universal satisfaction and pleasure, and with so much plaintive softness in the songs, that many Spaniards shed tears of joy at seeing the ability and skill of the little Indians.† One of these dramas, composed by priests in the Quichua language, is in my possession, and is a most valuable relic of those early efforts to introduce the miracle plays of Spain into Peru. ‡

* This dialect was called *Aymara* by the Jesuits at Juli, a blunder which is carelessly repeated by Garcilasso. The nature and origin of the mistake has been explained by me elsewhere.

† *G. de la Vega*, i. p. 204.

‡ The MS. was kindly presented to me by a Cura at Paucar-tambo in 1853. (See *Cuzco and Lima*, p. 190.) It is entitled, " *Usca Paucar, Auto Sacramental el Patrocinio de Maria, Señora Nuestra en Copacabana.*"

In his monstrous sentence in 1781, the Judge Areche prohibited "the representation of dramas, as well as all other festivals which the Indians celebrated in memory of their Yncas."* This proves that the ancient dramas of the Yncas were remembered and actually performed down to the year 1781; for those composed by Spanish priests ·cannot be intended, as they would not be prohibited by a Spanish judge.

These considerations will enable us to form an opinion of the antiquity of the drama of OLLANTA; which is now, for the first time, translated from Quichua into English.

The first printed mention of this most important relic of early American civilisation is to be found in a periodical published at Cuzco in 1837.† It is there stated that the drama was handed down by immemorial tradition, and that it was first committed to writing by Don Antonio Valdez, the Cura of Tinta, an intimate friend of the ill-fated Ynca Tupac Amaru, whose formidable insurrection was with difficulty suppressed by the Spaniards in 1780–81. The drama was frequently performed in presence of the Ynca Tupac Amaru. This account exactly coincides with the information I received in 1853 from Dr Don Pablo Justiniani, a descendant of the Yncas. He told me that the Cura of Tinta first reduced the drama to writing, and that the original manuscript was then in posses-

---

* "*Sentencia pronunciada en el Cuzco por el Visitador Don José Antonio de Areche, contra José Gabriel Tupac Amaru.*" This revolting but most curious and important state paper is published in vol. v. of the *Coleccion de obras y documentos*, by Don Pedro de Angelis. (Buenos Ayres, 1836–37.)

† "*Museo Erudito*," Nos. 5 to 9. Edited by Don José Palacios.

sion of his nephew and heir, Don Narciso Cuentas of Tinta. Dr Valdez, the Cura of Tinta, died at a great age in 1816.

Several copies were made from the original of Dr Valdez, for the lovers of Ynca lore, who abound in Cuzco, as well as in many a secluded town and village in the Peruvian Andes. Some extracts from the drama appeared in Peruvian newspapers, but the second notice of it (that in the *Museo Erudito* of Cuzco being the first) will be found in the *Antiguedades Peruanas* of Don Mariano Rivero and Dr Von Tschudi, which was published at Vienna in 1851.* It is curious that these authors should not have been acquainted with the article in the *Museo Erudito*, and with the fact that the drama was first committed to writing by Dr Valdez. They give two extracts from the drama in Quichua. The complete text in Quichua was first printed at the end of his *Kechua Sprache*, by Dr Von Tschudi, a work which appeared at Vienna in 1853.† This version is from a copy in the monastery of San Domingo at Cuzco, which is exceedingly corrupt; the copyist having modified what he could not read or understand as much as he thought proper, and having even introduced some Spanish words. In 1868 Don José Barranca published a Spanish translation of the Quichua drama of Ollanta.‡ He took the corrupt version of Von Tschudi for his text, but corrected many passages.

* P. 116.—*Antiguedades Peruanas, por Mariano Eduardo de Rivero y Juan Diego de Tschudi.*" (Vienne, 1851.)

† " *Die Kechua Sprache, por J. J. Von Tschudi,* ii. (Wien, 1853.)

‡ " *Ollanta ó sea la severidad de un padre y la clemencia de un rey drama traducido del Quichua al Castellano, con notas diversas, por José S. Barranca.*" (Lima, 1868.)

My own version of the drama was transcribed by myself, with great care, from the copy in possession of Dr Don Pablo Justiniani, the aged Cura of Laris, and a descendant of the Yncas. That copy was taken by his father, Don Justo Pastor Justiniani, from the original manuscript of Dr Valdez. I have collated my version with a copy in possession of Dr Rosas, Cura of Chinchero, and with the printed version in the *Kechua Sprache* of Dr Von Tschudi. The latter collation has convinced me of the genuine antiquity of the drama, for in every single instance where a corrupt or Hispanicised word or phrase occurs in the Von Tschudi version, I find classical Quichua in the version of Justiniani. This proves that all the corrupt forms in the Von Tschudi version arise from the carelessness of a copyist, and that they have no existence in the original document. In my account of the drama in *"Cuzco and Lima"* I gave some translated passages, which were made with the assistance of a young student of Cuzco, named Bernardo Puente de la Vega.*

The all-important question is whether the drama was handed down from the time of the Yncas, and merely committed to writing by Dr Valdez, who divided it into scenes, and inserted the stage directions; or whether Dr Valdez was the actual author, and composed the work himself in a classical and, in his day, almost archaic language. If the former opinion is the true one, the drama of OLLANTA is certainly the most important relic of ancient American civilisation; while in the latter case, though still an interest-

* Pp. 173-177, and 186.

ing specimen of Quichua composition, its great value and interest will be lost.

I was told by Dr Justiniani, and by other Quichua scholars whom I met at Cuzco in 1853, that the drama of Ollanta was undoubtedly ancient and composed before the Spanish conquest. Rivero and Von Tschudi also appear to have had no doubt upon this point, and Barranca strongly advocates the same view. But I was led, during my visit to Peru in 1860, to think that Dr Valdez was the author, though the drama might contain ancient songs and speeches, and though the plot was undoubtedly ancient.* I had not then carefully analysed the work itself. I have since done so, and this closer investigation has led me to revert to my earlier impression, and to concur with Justiniani, Rivero, Von Tschudi, and Barranca, that the drama is a pure relic of the ancient literature of the Yncas.

The internal evidence of the antiquity of the drama of Ollanta is, I consider, quite conclusive. We know from Garcilasso, that dramas were performed before the Yncas, and that the Indians had a special talent for acting; and we learn from the sentence of Areche that Quichua dramas were acted as late as 1781, to preserve the memory of the Yncas. They were performed before the ill-fated Tupac Amaru, whose intimate friend, Dr Valdez, committed the drama of Ollanta to writing, at about the time of the insurrection of the Ynca.† Thus we have a chain of evidence

---

* See my "*Travels in Peru and India*," p. 139 (note).

† For a narrative of the insurrection of Tupac Amaru, the last of the Yncas, in 1780-81, see my *Travels in Peru and India*, chap. ix. The

connecting the drama of Dr Valdez with the performance enacted before Tupac Amaru, the words of which had been orally transmitted from ancient Yncarial times. To these considerations are to be added the far more conclusive proofs of antiquity derived from the work itself. There is not a single modern or Spanish word or phrase in the whole work; nor is there the remotest allusion to Christianity or to any-thing Spanish. Moreover, the drama contains many words and grammatical forms, some of which I have indicated in the notes, that are archaic and long since disused. The only object of a Spanish priest, in composing such a work, would be to inculcate Catholic doctrine; and not to preserve the memory of ancient pagan rites in absolute purity. The Quichua play of *Usca Paucar*, in my possession, which was undoubtedly composed by a Spanish priest, contains many words that have been introduced since the conquest; and, though it is written in excellent Quichua, it does not contain one of the archaic grammatical forms that occur in Ollanta. If the latter work had been due to the authorship of Dr Valdez, it would have had some trace, however slight, of its Spanish origin; and would have resembled the miracle play of *Usca Paucar* in its general structure. The fact that OLLANTA is absolutely free from any indication of a Spanish touch, is a convincing proof that it is an ancient Ynca drama, handed down orally in order to be performed before the native chiefs, until 1780; and then committed to

texts of some of the official documents relating to the insurrection are printed in the collection of Angelis. Others, still in manuscript, are in my possession.

writing from the mouths of Indians by Dr Valdez, the friend
and sympathiser of the last of the Yncas. The old priest
merely made the divisions into scenes, which suggest themselves, and introduced the stage directions in accordance
with what he had himself seen, when the play was acted by
the Indians.

A knowledge of Ynca civilisation, derived from the pages
of Prescott, is sufficient for the appreciation of the argument
of this curious drama, which is as follows. The time is
placed in the reign of Pachacutec, an Ynca who flourished in
the latter part of the fourteenth century, whose numerous
reforms and conquests caused him to be remembered as one
of the most famous of the Peruvian sovereigns.* The hero
of the drama was a warrior named Ollanta, who was not
of the blood royal, but who nevertheless entertained a sacri-
legious love for a daughter of the Ynca, named Cusi Coyllur.
Ollanta is a word without special meaning in Quichua,† but
Cusi Coyllur means "the Joyful Star."‡ The play opens
with a dialogue between Ollanta and his servant, Piqui
Chaqui, a witty and facetious lad, whose punning sallies form

* *G. de la Vega*, ii. pp. 127–34, 145, 201–207. For his laws and
sayings, see pp. 207–10.

† Señor Barranca remarks that the word *Ollanta* has the form of the
accusative case, denoting that it is an incomplete part of a sentence.
He suggests that it may be a poetic form of *Ullata*, accusative of *Ullu*,
a word meaning the physical power of masculine love. He supposes
Ccahuari to be the word understood, which means *Behold!* The
name would thus be an expression of admiration for a manly lover.

‡ The Viceroy Toledo prohibited the Indians from giving the names
of the moon, stars, birds, animals, stones, serpents, or rivers, to their
children. *Ordenanzas*, lib. ii., tit. viii., ord. xiii. p. 144.

the comic vein which runs through the piece. Their talk is of Ollanta's love for the princess, and to them enters the High Priest of the Sun, who endeavours, by a miracle, to dissuade the audacious warrior from his forbidden love. In the second scene the princess herself laments to her mother the absence of Ollanta, and her father, the Ynca Pachacutec, expresses warm affection for his child. Two songs of undoubted antiquity are introduced; the first being a harvest song with a chorus threatening the birds that rob the corn, and the second being one of those mournful love-elegies which are peculiar to the Peruvian Indians. In the third scene Ollanta presses his suit upon the Ynca, is scornfully repulsed, and finally bursts out into open defiance, in a soliloquy of great force. Then there is an amusing dialogue with Piqui Chaqui, and another love song concludes the act. In the opening scene of the second act the rebellion of Ollanta is announced to the Ynca, and a general named Rumi-ñaui, or the "Stone Eyed,"* is ordered to march against him. The rebels hail the warrior Ollanta as their Ynca in the second scene, and prepare to resist the armies of Pachacutec; and in the third, Rumi-ñaui recounts the total defeat of himself and his armies by the rebel Ollanta. Meanwhile Cusi Coyllur had been delivered of a daughter, and for her crime she is immured in a dungeon of the convent of virgins, while her child, named Yma Sumac, is brought up in the same building without being aware of the existence of her mother. The long speech in which the child relates to her keeper the groans she

---

* A general under Atahuallpa had the same name; and it occurs, on two or three other occasions, in Ynca annals.

had heard in the garden, and the strange feeling with which they fill her mind, is considered by Señor Barranca to be the finest passage in the play. Then follows an amusing dialogue between Rumi-ñaui and the scrapegrace Piqui Chaqui, during which the death of the Ynca is announced. Pachacutec is succeeded by his son Ynpanqui, who had been absent for many years, engaged in the conquest of the coast valleys, and who is supposed to be imperfectly informed of the events that had taken place round Cuzco. He entrusted the command against the rebel to Rumi-ñaui, who adopted a cunning stratagem. Concealing his army in a neighbouring ravine, he came to the stronghold of the rebels, and appeared before Ollanta covered with blood, declaring that he had been cruelly treated by the new Ynca, and that he desired to join the insurrection. He encouraged Ollanta and his troops to celebrate the festival of the Sun with drunken orgies, and, when all were heavy with liquor, he admitted his own men and captured the whole of the rebels. In the first scene of the third act there is a touching dialogue between Yma Sumac and her governess Pitu Salla, which ends in the child being allowed to visit her mother in the dungeon. In the second scene the successful stratagem of Rumi-ñaui is related to the Ynca by a messenger, and Ollanta, and his companions, are brought in as prisoners, by the victorious general. The great rebel is not only pardoned by his magnanimous sovereign, but restored to all his honours; and in the midst of the ceremonies of reconciliation, the child Yma Sumac bursts into the presence, and entreats the Ynca Ynpanqui to save the life of his sister and her mother. The Ynca and his

nobles are conducted to the dungeon of Cusi Coyllur, who
was supposed to have been long since dead. The unfortunate
princess is restored to the arms of her lover, and receives the
blessing of the Ynca.

I have endeavoured to give the bare literal meaning of the
original, line by line, but it abounds in puns and double
meanings which cannot be re-produced. Yet an idea will
be conveyed to the mind of the reader, of the ancient
literature of the Yncas, and of the poetic faculty to which
they had attained, even by the present bald attempt at a
translation. The Quichua and English are given in parallel
columns. The different readings in the Von Tschudi version,
of which there are many, are given in italics, and the passages
in my version, which are omitted by Von Tschudi and
Barranca, are also indicated. I cannot hope that the translation is free from numerous mistakes. The value of the
present publication is that the text of an older and purer
version than that already given to the world in the *Kechua
Sprache* of Von Tschudi, will be preserved. The translation
is the result of much careful study; and it does, I believe, in
spite of many blunders which will doubtless be detected and
corrected by future students, give the general sense of the
original. Thus the purest and oldest text will now be
accessible to inquirers in this field of research, while the
translation will furnish additional material for judging of the
sort of civilisation that was developed in this part of South
America, before its discovery by Europeans. Such, at least,
is my aim in this effort to give the old Ynca Drama an
English dress.

The tradition at Cuzco in 1837, which was said to have been handed down in the families of the Caciques of Belen and San Blas, was that the drama was based on an historical event;* but this seems more than doubtful. The stronghold of the rebel is placed among the magnificent ruins in the vale of Vilca-mayu, which are now called Ollanta-tambo from the classical associations connected with the drama, but the greater part of the ruins is far more ancient than the time of Pachacutec. A detailed account of the ruins, and of the vale of Vilca-mayu, will be found in one of my former works on Peru.† A bust on an earthen vase was presented to Don Antonio Maria Alvarez, the political chief of Cuzco in 1837, by an Indian who declared that it had been handed down in his family from time immemorial, as the likeness of the general Rumi-ñaui, who plays an important part in the drama of Ollanta.‡ The person represented must have been a general, from the ornament on the forehead called *mascapaycha*, and wounds were cut in the face. This, so far as it goes, is a confirmation of the genuine antiquity of the drama. Internal evidence inclines me to fix its date, in the reign of the great Ynca Huayna Ccapec, about A.D. 1475 to 1525.§ Love is allowed to break through the rigid laws of the Ynca court to some extent; but otherwise the state of society, and the manners and customs met with in the drama, agree generally, but not so closely as to justify a suspicion of

---

* *Museo Erudito*, No 5, p. 9. † *Cuzco and Lima*, p. 179.
‡ *Museo Erudito*, No. 5.
§ For my reason for fixing this date, see note 66, at the end of this volume.

plagiarism, with those described by Garcilasso and other early Spanish writers.

The drama of Ollanta is not alone in allowing a romantic passion to transgress the usages of the Ynca court. A still more interesting love story is told by Balboa,* who relates the events as having actually occurred during the reign of Ynca Huascar, and as having been recounted to him by contemporaries. I mention it as a proof that the plot of Ollanta is not in opposition to probabilities; but space forbids the gratification of my natural wish to tell this second love tale of Ynca times.

I am in possession of twenty ancient Ynca songs, which I obtained from Dr Justiniani, and which had been first committed to writing in the last century by his grandfather and by Dr Valdez; and I also have some Quichua poems by Dr Lunarejo, the most elegant Quichua scholar of Spanish times. I hope hereafter to find time to complete the translation of these additional fragments of Ynca literature. Meanwhile I am fully persuaded that diligent research in the towns and villages of the Peruvian Andes would be rewarded by the discovery of further specimens of the ancient literature of the children of the Sun.

CLEMENTS R. MARKHAM.

August 1871.

---

* *Balboa*, cap. xvi. pp. 224-304.

APU OLLANTA AND CUSI COYLLUR.

A DRAMA OF THE YNCAS.

B

Dramatis Personæ.

THE YNCA PACHACUTEC.[1]

THE YNCA YUPANQUI,[2] *son of Pachacutec.*

OLLANTA,[3] *General of Anti-Suyu.*

RUMI-ÑAHUI,[4] *General of* { *Colla-Suyu.* *Hanan.*

UILLAC UMU,[5] *High Priest.*

URCO HUARANCCA,[6] *Follower of Ollanta.*

HANCO HUAYLLU, AUQUI,[7] *Old rebel.*

PIQUI CHAQUI,[8] *Servant of Ollanta.*

ANAHUARQUI,[9] *Queen.*

CUSI COYLLUR,[10] *Princess.*

YMA SUMAC,[11] *Daughter of Cusi Coyllur.*

CCACCA MAMA,[12] *Matron of the Virgins.*

PITU SALLA,[13] *a Virgin.*

Messengers, Princesses, Attendants. Young men and women dancing and singing, with music.

ACT I.

SCENE I.

Enter OLLANTA (*in a mantle fringed with gold bezants, and with a club over his shoulder*), *and his servant* PIQUI CHAQUI.

OLLANTA.

Piqui Chaqui ricunquichu
Cusi Coyllurtac huasinpi ?

Piqui Chaqui, hast thou seen
Cusi Coyllur in her house ?

PIQUI CHAQUI.

Ama Ynti munachunchu
Chayman churacunaitacca
Manachu ccanccu manchanqui
Incacc[14] ususin casccantacca ?

No ! The Sun would not permit
That I should go near it.
How is it that you have no fear,
She being daughter of the Ynca ?

OLLANTA.

Chaypas cachun, munasaccmi
Chay lulucusccay urpita[15]
Ñancay sonccoy paipaca chita
Paillallatan munascani !

In spite of that, I must ever love
That most tender turtle-dove.
My heart in that road
Alone desires to search.

PIQUI CHAQUI.

Supaycha raicus[16]-casunqui
Ycha ccancca muspha[17]quipas :

Supay must have bewitched you,
And you wander in your speech.

Hinantimpin huarma sipas	Are there not many other maidens
Anchatan rucupacunqui	That you can love before you are old ?
Yma ppunchaucha yachancca	The day that a knowledge of your love
Ynca yuyaycusccayquita	Shall come to the Ynca,
Ccorochinccan umayquita	He will have your head cut off,
Ccantacc canqui aycha canca.	And your body roasted like meat.

OLLANTA.

Ama runa, harccahuaichu !	Man ! hold me not,
Caipitacc sipirccoy quiman [18]	Or I will strangle thee !
Ama rimapayahuaychu	Talk not too much before me,
Maquiyhuantaccttiqquiquiman.	Or with my hand I will tear thee to pieces.

PIQUI CHAQUI.

Puriy ari aysarccamuy	Away then ! Let me be gone,
Allcco [19] huarmuscca hinata ;	And not fall like a dog.
Ychacca ama ñoccata	This shall not be for me.
Puriy, Piqui, mascarccamuy	Away Piqui ! He will seek me,
Nihuanquicha sapa huata	He shall miss me each year,
Sapa ppunchay, sapa tuta.	Each day, each night.

OLLANTA.

Ñan ñiquina, Piqui Chaqui,	Go then ! Piqui Chaqui,
Quiquin huañuy-ychunantin	Lead forth the dances of straw. [a]

Hinantin Urcco hinantin	For me though my enemies oppose me,
Sayaninman Aucca huaqui	Though a mountain obstruct
Chaypachapas, sayaymani	Yet will I encounter them.
Paycunahuan churaccuspa	I will risk all this,
Ñoccan y causay huamuspa	And risk life itself
Ccoyllurniypi mitccascani !	To embrace the Coyllur.

PIQUI CHAQUI.

Supay llocsimunman chayri ?	If Supay should stand in the way ?

OLLANTA.

Payta huanpas tustuymanmi.	Him also would I trample down !
(*Paytapas ñocca*)*	

PIQUI CHAQUI.

Mana cenccata ricuspan	You cannot see your own nose,
Cunan ccama rimascanqui.	And therefore you speak thus.

OLLANTA.

Chaypas, Piqui huillallahuay	Say then, Piqui !
Ama ymata pacaspayqui	Canst thou hide for me,
Manachu Ccoyllur ricusccayqui	So that Coyllur may see it,
Llapacc ttican ? y ñillahuay.	This flower ?

PIQUI CHAQUI.

Ccoyllurllahuan musphascanqui	Still mad about the Coyllur !
Manan ñocca ricunichu	I have never seen her.

* Interlined words in italics are the differences in Dr Von Tschudi's version.

Paycha canccan, ycha pichu
Ccayna ppuncha ranqui ranqui
Pununtas qquecuna uccupi
Lloccsimuriccan chay Surupi
Ynti manri ricchacunccan
Quillamantacc tucupunccan[20]

Who, with other spotless ones,
Came forth but yesterday?
Perchance it was she!
Beautiful as the morning,
Brilliant as the Sun in his course,
Bright as the moon.

OLLANTA.

Paypunin chaycca riccsinqui
Yma sumac, yma cusi
Cunallanmi purininqui

Cunaiñiyhuan cusi cusi.

No doubt it was she,
How lovely! how joyful!
But now you must have walked
     by her!
How bright and joyful is she!

PIQUI CHAQUI.

Mana ñoccacca riymachu
Ppunchaycca hatun huasita
Chaypiñatacc ccepintinta[21]

Mana pita reccsiymanchu.

Indeed I cannot speak of her.
I cannot go this day to her
     house,
They would not let a porter in,
And I know her not by sight.

OLLANTA.

Reccsimiñan ñinquitaccmi?

Did you not say that you knew
     her?

PIQUI CHAQUI.

Chaytacca ñiyllama ñimi
Tutallan ccoyllurcca ccanchan,

Tutallatacc mi reccsini.

I said that, meaning
That as the stars shine at night
     in their places,
So I only know her at night.

OLLANTA.

Lloccsihuay caymanta laicca[22]	Be gone then, wizard.
Chay ccoyllur munacusccaicca	My adored Cusi Coyllur
Ynticc cayllanpi ashuanta	Is more bright than the Sun,
Ccanchan chipchin sapanmanta	She has no rival.

PIQUI CHAQUI.

Chaycca cunan llocsimuscan	If it should be possible
Huc machu ycha payachu	I will look out for some old man or woman,
Huarmi mami ricchacuscan	I will be awake and try it.
Ycha cunainyqui apacchu	I will convey you to her
Payhuan cunay ñoccatacca	And speak with her.
Cachapuni [23] ñihuanmanri	I will consent to be your messenger,
Pi may caccpas huacchatacca.	Though I am but a poor man.

Enter UILLAC UMU,[24] *gazing on the Sun, wearing a black "uncu,"
and with a knife in his hand.*

UILLAC UMU.

Causacc Ynti, yupiquitan	O living Sun! I watch thy course
Ullpuycuspa yupaychani	As thou marchest onwards.
Ccan pacctaccmi huaccaychani	For thee are now preparing
Huarancca llama hinatan.	A thousand llamas
Ppunchaynipi cconospa	For the day of thy festival.
Yahuarñinta ccaillai pi	Their blood shall flow in thy presence.

Ninapi canaspa llipi	For thee are they destroyed in the fire,
Rupachincca mana accospa.	And shall burn, after the fast is over.

OLLANTA.

Piqui Chaqui, caycca hamuscan	See who comes, Piqui Chaqui !
Chay Amauta, Uillac Umu !	It is the wise Uillac Umu.
Yma qquenchas manu ccumu	Behold this lion is coming
Payhuan cusca purimuscan	Accompanied by evil omens :
Checcnicunin cay layccata	I hate this soothsayer
Ancha llaquita huatuccnin	Who, ever when he speaks,
Tucuy phutita huatucctin.	Announces black auguries.

PIQUI CHAQUI.

Upallay ama rimaychu	Hush. Speak not !
Payni huc rimasccayquita	Even now that sorcerer
Nan yachaña yscay mitta	Knows twice as much as you
Nan huatuna chaychu caychu.	Concerning what you said.

OLLANTA.

Ricuanman rimaycusacc	I will speak ; now that he has seen me.
Ccapac Auqui, Uillac Umu	O powerful and noble Uillac Umu,
Yupaychayquin pachaccuti	I adore thee with profound veneration.
Cccapac cachun tucuy sutti	From thee nothing is hidden
Hinatintacc Ccapac ccumu.	We see that all must be known to thee.

Uillac Umu.

Ccapac Ollantay ccapaccpas	O valiant Ollanta!
Tucuy Suyu ttaccta cachun	The province is at thy feet.
Callpay quitacc puchu cachun	Thy valour suffices
Llapata Secc-ñanapaccpas.	To subdue all things.

Ollanta.

Anchatan manchani cucun	I tremble to see thee here,
Machuita caypi ricuspa	And to behold before me
Hinatinmi chiri uspa	These cold ashes,
Fica, ttunu, ccacca runcu	Flowers, vases, bags of coca,
Maypachas ccanta ricuncu.	As many as approach, wonder at these things.
Ñihuai imapactac caicca	Tell me! for what are they intended?
Ynca chu huacc yanccasunqui	Is it for the Ynca thou preparest
Llaquichu pusamisunqui	To discover evil omens
Icha cusipacchu chaicca?	By the spider divination?
Ymamantac ccan hamunqui	For what purpose dost thou come,
Manarac raymi cactincca.	Seeing that the Raymi [b] is not yet?
Onccorinchu icha Ynca	Is, peradventure, the Ynca sick?
Imatachu huatuncanqui	How dost thou make thy divi-
(*Ccanllachu huatupacunqui*)	nations?
Yahuar sutucc panti tunqui?[25]	By the blood drops of the Tunqui?[c]
Ynti huatana ppunchaupas	The day of observing the Sun,
Quilla macchina pachapas	The sacrifices of the Moon
Ancha caruraccmi cascan	Are still very far off.

Chairacmi quillata pascan	The month has not yet commenced,
Situa Raymi cañampacpas	Of the Situa Raymi.[d]
(*Hatun Ccocho.*)	

UILLAC UMU.

Anyaspachu tapuhuanqui	Why dost thou ask me reproachfully ?
Huarmaiquichu icha cani ?	Am I not thy servant ?
Tucuy ymatan yachani	I know all things
Canña ricuy yuiahuanqui.	As thou but now remindedst me.

OLLANTA.

Mancharinmi llaclla souccoy	My coward heart trembles
Yancca ppunchaupi ricuspa	To see thee on a special day,
Chayamuiñiqui ruruspa	That I may benefit by thy coming,
Ychapas ñocapac onccoy.	Even when a sickness is the result.

UILLAC UMU.

Ama Ollantay manchaichu	Fear not, Ollanta,
Cunan caipi ricuhuaspa	At seeing me here,
Ychapas ccanta munaspa	For, in truth, it is because I love thee.
Punimuni pahuacc huaichu	I will fly, where thou likest, as straw before the wind. Tell me the thoughts
(*Phahuamuni huaira ichu*)	
Ñihuay ama pacahuaichu	
(*yuyainiquipichu*)	
Ymatan tocellan souccoyqui	That find a place in thine heart.
(*Caman chai saccra*)	

Cay ppunchaymi campac ccoi- qui	This day I will give thee
Sami miuta acllacuita	The choice of poison or fortune,
Causay huañuya taricuyta	That between life and death
Chaitan cunan horccomuyqui.	You may make your choice.

OLLANTA.

Asuan sutinta mastarei	Explain more clearly
Chay huatuscaiqui simita	Now that thou hast divined.
Cai anhuiscca ccaitutari (quipuscca)	Say what are on the quipus
Pascarei asuan pharita.	With more quickness.

UILLAC UMU.

Ccaicca Ollantay uyapay	Here thou hast, O Ollanta!
Yachaiñispa tariscanta	What I have divined.
Yachascanin llapallanta	I only know all things,
Pacasccata ñoca sapay	I know even
Cantaccmi ñocacpas callpas	What is most hidden.
Ccan Auquita horcconaipac	I am able to make thee Auqui.ᶜ
Huarmamantan uyhuarccayqui	As I have nourished thee,
[Anchatatac munancayqui]	And loved thee much,
Camancani yananaypac	I ought to aid thee
(y cunanpas)	
Anti-suyu camachictan	To become ruler over Anti-suyuſ
Tucuy ccanta ricsisunqui	Thou art known to all.
Ccantan Ynca munasunqui	The Ynca loves thee
Llautunta²⁶ ccanhuanmi checc- tan	Even to dividing with thee the llautu.

Hinantinta ccahuaricctan | Among all—he has chosen thee,
Ñahuinta ccampi churarcan : | Putting his eyes on thee
Callpaiquita pucararccan | He will increase thy forces
Auccancunac champinpaccpas | That thou mayest resist his enemies.

Tucuy ima haicca caccpas | Whatever thing may exist
Ccanllallapin puchucarccan | With thy presence it shall cease.
Chaychu cunan phiñachista | Answer me now
Sonccoiquipi yuyascanqui ? | Even when thy heart is appeased.

(tocllascanqui ?[27]) | (Caught as with a lasso.)
Ususintan ccan munanqui | Dost thou not desire his daughter,

Chay Ccoyllurta musphachista | That maddening Coyllur,
Chay cusita urmacheita | That Cusi, that she may fall.
Ama chaytaccan ruraychu | Refrain from this !
Amapuni cururaychu | Do not commit this crime.
Sonccoyquipi chay huchata : | Keep thy heart from it.
Munasunqui pay anchata | Though she loves thee much,
Manan chay camasunquichu | Do not thus with her soul.
Chaichica cuyascanmanchu | Do not act in this way,
Chay quellita cutichihuac ? | Do not commit this crime,
Mitcaspachu purinihuac | Showing such ingratitude
Urmahuac huc pponcomanchu? | In return for great favours !
Manan Ynca munanmanchu | The Ynca will not suffer it,
Anchatan Ccoyllurta cuyan | For he loves the Coyllur.
Rimarinqui chayri cunan | If you should speak of it,
Ttocyanccan phiñaricuspa | His rage will be great.
Ccantac ricuy muspha muspha | Are you becoming mad

Auquimanta cahuac runan ?	At having been created an Auqui ?

OLLANTA.

Maymantatac can yachanqui	How knowest thou this
Cay sonccoypi pacascayta ?	Which is hidden in my heart ?
Mamallanmi yachan chayta	Her mother only knows it ?
Cunantac ccam huillahuanqui.	How is it that you now reveal it ?

UILLAC UMU.

Quillapin tucuy ymapas	All that has ever happened
Suyuscca quipu ñocapac	Is present to me, as on a quipu,
(*Seqquesca quellca* [28])	
Asuan pacascayqui caccpas	Even what thou hast hidden most
Sutillanmi can ñocapac.	To me is clear.

OLLANTA.

Huatuscarccanmi sonccoypi	My heart tells me
Ñocac miuy canayquita	That I myself have produced
Chaquisca upyanayquita	The poison which, thirsting, I drank.
Huicchuhuacchu huc onccoypi!	Wilt thou abandon me in this evil case ?

UILLAC UMU.

May chica cutin upyanchis	How often do we drink
Ccori querupi huañuyta	Death from a vase of gold.
Yuyariey tucuy hamuita	Remember that all comes to us,
Ricuy huallahuisan canchis.	And we are rash.

OLLANTA.

Huc camallaña ccorohuay	Behold ! thou now hast
Chay tumiqui maquiquipin	Thy knife in thy hand,
Cai sonccoyta ccan horccohuay	Cut out my heart,
Chaipac cani chaquiquipin.	I am here, at thy feet.

UILLAC UMU (*To* PIQUI CHAQUI).

Chaccay tticata apamuy !	Bring me that flower !
Ña ricunqui chaquis caccta	Behold that it is dry.
Hina chaquin huc nanaccta	Yet though it be dry
Unuta huaccancca. Hamuy.	It shall drop water. Behold !
	[*Presses it, and water flows out.*

OLLANTA.

Asuan utccaytan huc caca	More easily might a rock
Unuta pharara rancca	Pour forth water,
Huaccueta pacha huaccanca	More easily might the earth weep,
Mana ñocachu pacpaca	Than that I should abandon
Ccoyllurta mana ricusac.	The Coyllur.

UILLAC UMU.

Chay allpaman huc ruracta (*topoman*)	Sow seeds on this earth
Churaycuy ccañan ricunqui	And thou shalt see at once
Manaraccha ripucunqui	They will multiply ;
Mirauccan caru caruta	Increasing more and more
Llinpanccan chay toputapas	And exceeding the size of the field,

Hinan huchayqui puriscan

Hinan pisipanqui campas.

So will thy crime increase

Until it shall overwhelm thee.

OLLANTA.

Huc camaña huillascayqui

Pantascayta hatun Yaya [29]

At once thou hast shown me,

O great Father! that I have erred!

Cunan yachay, yachay ccaya

Hucllamantan arhuihuanqui

Now I know it, I know it!

Now thou hast surprised me in it,

Hatunmi arhuihuay huascca

The lasso that surrounds me is great,

Ranccucunaypac huatascca

(*Seccoconaipac*)

I might hang myself with it.

Chaypas ccori caytumanta

Simpasca cay hinamanta

    (*chaicca caimautan,*)

Ccori hucha sipsicasca

Though it be plaited with gold,

This unequalled crime—

A golden crime will be my executioner:

Cusi Ccoyllurca huarmiyñan

Pay huan huat asccañan cani

Paychu cunan yahuar sani

Ñocapas paipa saphiuñan

Mamanpas yachan y ñinñan

If Cusi Coyllur is my wife,

I am lassoed with her,

I am now of her blood,

I am of her lineage,

As her mother knows and will declare.

Yucata rimaycuy sihuay

Yanapahuay pusarihuay

Cay Ccoyllurta ccohuanampac

Help me to speak to the Ynca,

Accompany me to him

That he may give Cusi Coyllur to me.

Calpaypas asta camampac	I will seek her with all my power.
Piñacuctin puriy sihuay	Present me to him, though he is enraged,
Anchatachus usnchihuañman (millahuanman)	Though he should despise me
Mana Ynca yahuar cactiy?	For not being of Ynca blood,
Ñaupac huiñayniyta ccatiy	When he beholds my youth
Ychapas chaypi urmanman	Perhaps that will be a defect.
Ccahuarichuu mitcascayta	He will count my faults
Yuparichun purisccayta	And examine my paces.
Cay champiypin ricurincca	He can look upon my battle-axe
Nanacc huaranca huarminca (Millai)	Which has humbled thousands,
Chaquinman ullpuchiscayta.	And brought them to my feet.

Uillac Umu.

Chicallata Auqui rimay!	Dost thou speak thus, O Auqui!
Cai chutquicca ancha ashuisc-can	Thy shuttle is broken,
Cai ccaitu millay pitisccan	The thread is torn asunder,
Can ttisanqui cam cururay	The wool and card are broken.
Sapa Yncata rimaycamuy (Yncanchista)	Wouldst thou speak to the Sole Ynca?
Sapampi llaquic phutispa (millai)	For all your sorrow
Pisillata rimarispa	Thou hast little to say.
Allintarac ricucamuy	Reflect well that where I am

Ñocaca maipi caspapas   I shall always be bound
Yuyasccayquin sipisccapas.   To repress thy thoughts.

                                                    [*Exit.*

Ollanta.

Ollantay ccarim carqui   Ollanta ! thou art a man !
Ama ymata manchaychu   Thou hast valour.
Ama chailla anchayaichu.   Thou hast no fear.
(*Ccampac pisipan manchaichu*)
Ccanmi Ccoyllur ccancha-huan-   Coyllur, it is thee I must pro-
    qui   (*llanta*)   tect.
Piqui Chaqui maypincanqui ?   Piqui Chaqui, where art thou ?

Piqui Chaqui.

Puñurccusani nanacctan   I have slept like a stone,
Tapiapacmi mosccocuni.   And have dreamt bad dreams.

Ollanta.

Ymata ?   What ?

Piqui Chaqui.

Huc atoccta [30] huatasccata.   Of a fox tied up.
    (*asnuta*)*
    (*llamata*)†   ### Ollanta.
Ccanpunim chaycca carcanqui.   Certainly thou art the fox.

Piqui Chaqui.

[Chaycha chuñuyan senccaypas]‡   Therefore my nose scents better,
Chaycha huiñancay rincripas.   Therefore my ears grow longer.

---

* Von Tschudi.   † Barranca's correction of Von Tschudi.
‡ The passages between brackets [   ] are not in Von Tschudi.

                                                    c

OLLANTA.

Hacu, Ccoyllurman pusahuay.	Let us go. Take me to the Coy-llur.

PIQUI CHAQUI.

Ppunchayracmi.	It is still daylight.

                                           [*Exeunt.*

SCENE II.—INTERIOR OF THE ACLLA-HUASI.

Enter CUSI COYLLUR *weeping, and her mother the* CCOYA.

CCOYA.

Haicacmantan chica llaqui	Since when hast thou been so sad,
Cusi Ccoyllur, yntic rirpun ?[31]	O Cusi Coyllur! image of the sun ?
Haycac-mantan chincaripun	Since when hast thou aban-doned
Cusihuan samihuan huaqui ?	All thy pleasures, all thy joy ?
Huccu siquicuna paraspa	A deep sadness afflicts
Sonccollaytan sipin ccaña	My sorrowing heart.
Huañuy llayman huc camaña	I would rather face death
Chica pputita ccahuaspa	Than witness such misery.
Ollantaytan munarccanqui	Dost thou love Ollantay ?
Ña taccmi payhuan yanasca	Art thou his companion ?
Huarmiña canqui huatascca ?	Art thou now his wife ?
Ccantacmi aclla curccanqui	Hast thou selected
Ccosayquipac chay Auqui ?	This Auqui for thy husband ?

[Cusitaccmi maquiquita
Huayhuarccanqui pacchas-
  chita?]
Samaricuy asllallata.

Rest thyself a little.

CUSI COYLLUR.

Ay Ccoya! Ay Mamallay!
(*Ñustallay!*)
Ymaynam mana huaccasac
Ymaynam mana sullasac
Ychay Auqui munasccallay
Ccaca tupu huayllusccallay
(*Ychay ccacca*)
Cai chica tuta ppunchaupi

Cai chica huarma casccaypi
Y cconccahuan y haqquehuan
Y uyayta pay ppaquihuan
Mana huaturicuhuaspa
Ay Mamallay! Ay Ccoyallay!
  (*Ñustallay*)
Ay huayllucuscay ccosallay!
Canta ricsicunay paccha
Quillapi chay yana ppacha,
Ynti pas pacaricuspa
Ccospapurccan chiri uspha
Phuyupas tacru ninahuan
Llaquita pailla huillahuan
Accochinchay [32] llocsimuspa
(*Ccollurpas chasca tucuspa*)

Ah my Queen! Ah my mother!

How should I not weep!
How should I not mourn!
If my beloved Auqui,
If my revered guardian,

During all these days and
  nights,
In this my tender age
Forgets and forsakes me.
He turns away his face
And has not asked for me.
Ah my mother! Ah my Queen!

Ah my beloved husband!
From the day that I came here
The moon has been darkened,
The sun is obscured
As if covered with ashes.
A stormy cloud appeared
To announce my sorrow,
The bright comet was darkened.

Chupata aysaricuspa	Its tail departed.
Tucuyñincu tapya carccan	All things are against me,
Phuya yahuarta paraccan	The clouds rain blood.
(*Hinantipas pisiparccan*)	
Ay Ccoyallay ! Ay Mamallay !	Ah my Queen ! Ah my mother !
(*Ñustallay*)	
Ay huayllucusccay ccosallay !	Ah my beloved husband !

Enter the YNCA PACHACUTEC, *with Attendants.*

CCOYA.

Picharicuy uyayquita	Wash thy face,
Chaquichicuy [33] ñahuiquita.	Dry thine eyes.
(*richei*)	
Ynca yayayquim llocismun	The Ynca, thy father comes,
Caiñecmanmi cutirimun.	Behold him approaching. Turn to him.

YNCA PACHACUTEC.

Cusi Coyllur soncco ruru	Cusi Coyllur ! Fruit of my heart !
Llipi churicunac ttican	Bright flower among my children !
Cay ccascoypa panti llican	Fair net around my breast !
Simiquin raurac huayruru	Warm sweetness to my mouth !
(*Cay cuncaipac cay huaisuru*)	
Cay ccascoyman hanucy urpi	Come, my dove, to my bosom !
Cay ricraypi samaricuy	Rest here in my arms !
Cay ñahuiypi pascaricuy	Open thine eyes to me,

Ccori llica canti ucupi	And unreel the golden thread
(*curur*)	within.
Tucuy llumpac sami ccanpin	In thee I have my delight,
Ñahuiypa lirpunmi canqui	Thou art the apple of my eye—
Ñahuiyquipin huanqui huanqui	Thou art to me my eye.
Tucuy Ynticc huachin champin	Here thou hast the club of the Ynca,
Llipitan llican ñahuiyqui	And with a look thou commandest it.
Quechip nayquita quichaspa	Who can open thy bosom
(*Pichu ccaraiquita*)	
Simiquitari pascaspa	To discover thy thoughts
Pupantacmi samayñiqui	And secure thy content ?
Ccanllan canqui yayayquipac	Thou art to thy father
Tucuy samin causayhuanpas	The only hope of his life.
Ñoccata ricuspa campas	Thy presence is to me
Causay huiñay cusinaypac.	A life-time of endless joy.

CUSI COYLLUR.

Muchanin huarancca cuti	I adore thee a thousand times.
	[*Kneels to the Ynca.*
Llampu Yoyay chaquiquita	Here, O my Father, at thy feet,
Llantuhuay churiquita	Oh show favour to thy child,
(*huarancca mitta*)	
Chincarichun tucuy phuti.	And drive off my sorrows.

YNCA PACHACUTEC.

Ccan chaquipi, ccan ullpuspa*	Thou at my feet ! Thou humbled !

* Ullpuycuspa.

Manchaspan cayta rimani !	I speak with astonishment !
Ccahuariy yayayquin cani	Remember that I am thy father,
Huihuayquin ccanta luluspa.*	I have cherished thee with tender care.
Huaccanquichu ?	Dost thou weep ?

CUSI COYLLUR.

Ccoyllurpas huaccan sullantan	Coyllur will weep like the dew
Yntin llocsinimuctincca	That is driven away by the sun.
Sullani unun purincca	I bedew with water that departs,
Mayllarincca chay sullatan.	And I will wipe away the dew.
(*Macc-chirincca* †)	

YNCA PACHACUTEC.

Hamuy munacusccay, halla,	Come, my beautiful love,
Tianicuy cay arpaypi.	And sit down by my side.
	[*She sits down at his feet.*

Enter Servants.

Huarmayquicunan hamusca	The servants come
Ccanta cusichicunanpacc.	To do thy pleasure.

YNCA PACHACUTEC.

Yaycuy camuchucu ñiy.	Let them enter.

---

* Llullucuspa.

† Tschudi says, in a note, that this is unintelligible to him.

Enter young Indians dancing, with small drums.　Music within.
They sing.

Song.

Ama piscu miccuychu	Bird, forbear to eat,
Tuyallay.[34]	O my Tuya !
Ñustallaipa chacranta	The crop of my Princess,
Tuyallay.	O my Tuya !
Manan hina tucuichu	Do not thus rob,
Tuyallay.	O my Tuya !
Hillucunan saranta	The maize which is green,
Tuyallay.	O my Tuya !
Panaccaymi rurunri	The fruit is soft inside,
Tuyallay.	O my Tuya !
Ancha cconi munispa	Though truly the rind is thick,
(*ccari murirpas*)	O my Tuya !
Tuyallay.	
Ñucñuracmi ucunri	The leaves are tender,
Tuyallay.	O my Tuya !
Llulluracmi raphinpas	Do not perch on them,
(*Quequeracmi*)	O my Tuya !
Tuyallay.	
Huaranccanan hilluta	Do not be very greedy,
Tuyallay.	O my Tuya !
Pupasccayquin ccantapas	Or thou shalt be trapped,
Tuyallay.	O my Tuya !
[Cuchusaccmi silluta]	Thy nails shall be cut,
Tuyallay.	O my Tuya !

[Happiscayquin ccantapas
(*Pupascayquin*)   Tuyallay.

And thou shalt be caught,
    O my Tuya!

Piscucata huatucuy

Seize that little bird,

    Tuyallay.

    O my Tuya!

Sipisccata ccahuariy

Fasten him with a collar,

    Tuyallay.

    O my Tuya!

Sonccollanta tapucuy

Make his heart beat,

    Tuyallay.

    O my Tuya!

Phuruntatac mascariy

Seek him out and secure him,

    Tuyallay.

    O my Tuya!

Hinasccatan ricunqui
(*Lliquisccatan*)

You will see how he is treated,

    Tuyallay.

    O my Tuya!

Huc ruruta chapchactin

When he touches a grain,

    Tuyallay.

    O my Tuya!

Hinatacmi ricunqui

You will see how he is treated,

    Tuyallay.

    O my Tuya!

[Huellallapas chincacctin

When one is missing,

    Tuyallay.]

    O my Tuya!

YNCA PACHACUTEC.

Cusicuscay Cusi Ccoyllur
Huarmay quicunac chaupinpi
Cay mamayquipa huasimpi.

Enjoy thyself, Cusi Coyllur,
In the midst of thy maidens,
In the house of thy mother.

    [*Exit.*

CCOYA.

As ñucñuta taquipuychis
Amauta parahuicc cuna
(*Munacusccai sicllaicuna*)

Sing with more sweetness,
Loveable nymphs,

Tap-yatan taquin cay cuna	Depart, you that have sung of misfortune;
Ccancunari chay ripuychis.	Let us have other music.
	[*Music within.*

Song.

Yscay munaracuc urpi [35]	Two loving turtle doves
(*Yscay munacusccai*)	
Llaquin, phutin, anchin, huaccan	Are sad, mourn, sigh, and weep.
Accoy raquis aucca ttacan	Both were buried in the snow.
(*Yscainintas ccasa pacan*)	
Huc chaqui mullpa curcupi	And a tree without verdure was their hard resting-place.
Hucñin cacsi chincachisca	One lost her companion
Huayllucuscan Pitullanta	And set out to seek her.
Huc socyapi sapalanta	She found her in a stony place,
Ccampanmanascca llaquiscca	But she was dead.
(*Mana haicac cachariscca*)	And sadly she began to sing,
Huacacc urpitacmi llaquin	My dove! where are thine eyes,
Pitullanta ccahuarispa	And where thy loving breast?
Huañuscataña tarispa	Where thy virtuous heart
Cay simipi paypac taquin	That I loved so tenderly?
Maymi Urpi chay ñahuiqui	Where, my dove! are thy sweet lips
Chay ccasccoyqui munaymunay	That divined my sorrows?
Chay sonccoyqui ñucñucunay	I shall suffer a thousand woes,
Chay achan ccanay simiqui?	Now my joys are ended.
(*llampu huatuc*)	And the unhappy dove
Chicachicuc cac urpiri	Wandered from sorrow to sorrow.
Ccacca ccaccapi musphaspa	Nothing consoled her

Huequenhuan ccaparcac chaspa	Or calmed her grief.
Quiccaman ñatac puririn	When the morning dawned
Hininantta tapucuspa	In the pure blue of heaven
Yanallay maypitac canqui	Her body reeled and fell,
(*Sonccollay*)	
Ñispan mitcan ranqui ranqui	And in dying she drew
Ñispan huañun ullpuycuspa.	A sigh all full of love.

Cusi Coyllur.

Chicantan ñin chay yarahui !	This yarahui[36] speaks truly.
Chicallataña taquihuay	Enough of music,
[Sapaytaña haqquehuaychis]	Torrents of tears,
Llocllarichuña cay ñahui.	Overflow mine eyes.

[*Exeunt.*

SCENE III.

Enter the Ynca Pachacutec, Ollanta, *and* Rumi-Ñahui.[5]
The Ynca *sits on his tiana.*

Ynca Pachacutec.

Cunan ppunchaumi Auqui cuna	Hail, O Auquis !
Ancha chariocc rimananchis	I declare the time has come
(*Ccan cunahuan*)	
Ñan chirau chayamuanchis[37]	For the army to prepare
Llocisnanñan llapa runa	For the road
Colla-sayun mascamuna.	To Colla-suyu.
(*Ccoya*)	
Ñan Chayanta camaricun	Chayanta is prepared
(*Ñas*)	

Ñocanchishuan llocsinampac	To join with us.
[Callpancuta tupunanpacc]	Our strength is immense.
Llapa llancus tacuricun	Let the arms be ready
Huachincuta thuparicun.	And the arrows sharpened.

OLLANTA.

Ymatas, Ynca, tacyanaca	How, O Ynca, are these cowards
Chay llaclla runacunaca	To be maintained by us?
(*haucca*)	
Cuzcohuanmi orco caicca	Cuzco and its mountains
Paycunapaca sayancca	Will rise against them;
Ñan pusac chunca huaranca	As well as eighty thousand men
Huallahuisa suyuscanña	Who wait, and are ready
Huancaniypa tocyananta	At the sound of the drum,
Pututuypa huaccananta	And at the blowing of the trumpet.
Ñan macana tuprasccaña	As for me my axe is sharp
Champipas camarisccaña.	And my club is chosen.
(*ñan acllasccaña*)	

YNCA PACHACUTEC.

Tucuytarac huacyay cunay	Still I will give my orders
Huillanquichisrac pactapas	That all shall assemble,
Cumuycunman huaquillanpas	For there may be many
Yahuarñincun ancha cuyay.	Who love their blood too well.

RUMI-ÑAHUI.

Ancha phiñas huñucuncu	To order and oblige
Yuncacunata huacyaspa	The Yuncas to work

Ñancunatari pascaspa	At clearing the roads
Ccaramantas uncu cuncu	And to dress in skins :
Hinan manchayñinta pacan	The most valiant
Chay pisi soncco Chayanta	In Chayanta might be ordered
Mana chaquic chayamanta	To assemble. I believe
Ñanta pascascca munascan	That this will show their cowardice,
Ñan accoya camariscca	Not wishing to march on foot.
Llamanchispas chacnanapac.	Now that the beasts are ready,
Acco punin ticranapac	We can march to battle,
Ñan ricranchis camarisca.	For our army is ready.

Ynca Pachacutec.

Llocsiytañachu yuyanqui	Dost thou think to go forth
Phiña amaru tincuric	To encounter them, as a fierce serpent,
Chay runacuna tacuric ?	And that thou wilt raise those people ?
Ñaupactarac ccan huacyanqui.	Thou shalt first appeal to them
Misqui simi payaynata	With a sweet mouth,
Ccuyanin ricuy runata	And show them compassion,
Manan yahuar hichaytachu.	Not shedding any blood
Pitapas ccollochiytachu.	And destroying no one.
(*Ni pita*)	

Ollanta.

Ñan ñoccapas llocsisacña	I too must march.
Tucuy iman camariscca	All things are prepared,
Soncco llami manchariscca	But my heart trembles,
(*Cai sonccoimi*)	
Huc yuyaypin musphasccaña	Maddened by one thought.

YNCA PACHACUTEC.

Rimariy ñiy cay llautuyta munaspapas.	Speak! I grant even my royal *llautu.*

OLLANTA.

Sapayquipi uyarihuay.	Hear me, alone.

YNCA PACHACUTEC.

Hanansuyu apu huarancca (*huamincca*)	General of Hanan Suyu
Huasiquipi samarimuy;	Rest in thy house,
Rima nanchisana cacctinca (*Ñocca huacyanai captincca*) Ccaya ppunchau muyurimuy.	I will call thee to-morrow.

RUMI-ÑAHUI.

Ccampa simiquin ñocapac	Thy word is mine;
Hunttaña huc chinlliyllapi.	I comply on the instant.
	[*Exit.*

OLLANTA.

Nan yachanqui Ccapac Ynca	Well thou knowest, Ccapac Ynca,
Huarmanantan yanasccayqui	That I have followed thee from childhood;
Ccantan huiñay ccahuancayqui	I have ever sought thy welfare,
Cay runasccayqui huamincca (*Rurarccaiqui cai*)	Showing my valour for thee,
Ccanta ccatispan callpaypas	To impose thy sway
Huaranccaman cutipurccan	Upon thousands of people.

Hampiypas umi sururccan
(*ccampai*)
Ccan raycutaccmi canipas.
Purun auccapas carccani

For thee have I sweated,

Ever have I lived to serve thee ;
I have been the terror of thy enemies.

Tucuy ccahuac tucuy tactac

Never have I failed to fall upon them,

Manchaciñinmi llapi llactac
Anta champin circarcani
Maypin manapas llocllacchu

And to conquer their towns
As with a brazen club.
Where have I not poured out torrents

Auccayquicunac yahuarnin ?
Pi pacmi mana chahuariñin
Ollantaypa sutin cacchu ?
Ñocan campa chaquiquiman
Hanan-suyu llipintinta

Of the blood of thine enemies?
Upon whom have I not imposed
The name of Ollanta ?
I have brought to thy feet
The bright hosts of Hanan-suyu,

Churasccani Yuncantinta
Yanayquipac huasiquiman
Chanca cunata canaspa
Raprancutan cuchurccani
Ñocatac cururarccani
Huanca Uillcata tactaspa.³ᵘ
Maypin mana sayarircan
Ollantay ñaupac ñaupacta ?

Thousands of Yuncas*ʰ*
As servants in thy house.
Conquering the Chancas*ⁱ*
I have made them submit.
I it was who conquered
The great Huanca Uillca,*ʲ*
Placing him at thy feet.
When has not Ollanta been first ?

Ñocaraycu tucuy llacta
Chaquiquiman hamurircan :
Ñarac llamputa llullaspa

I have added many villages
To thy dominions.
Now I have used persuasion,

Ñarac phina ccaparispa

Now I have resorted to force,

Ña yahuarniyta hichaspa

Now have I poured out blood,

Ñarac huañuyta tarispa

Now have I exposed myself to death.

Canmi yaya, ccohuarcanqui

Thou, my Father, hast bestowed

Ccori champita cantaccmi

This mace of gold

Ccori chuccuta ymapacmi

And this golden helm.

Auquimanta horccohuarcanqui?

Didst thou not raise me to be an Auqui?

(*Runa*)

Ccampan cay ccori macana

From thee is this golden club,

Ccampactacmi yma ccasccaipas

For thee shall be my prowess

Callpaypas chanincachun chaypas

And all that my valour gains.

Tucuytan chaypi mascana

Thou hast raised me

Ñan Aputa horccohuanqui

To be the fortunate chief

Anti-suyu huaminccata

Of Anti-suyu. From thee

Pisca chunca huaranccata

I command fifty thousand

Rurayquita yupahuanqui

Men who obey me,

Hinantin Anti ccatihuan

With all the Anti-suyu.

Ccanta yana ccuscallaypi

For all the services I have performed

Ñoccatahuanmi churayqui

I approach thee,

Ullpuycuspa chaquiquiman

And humble myself at thy feet

Asllatahuan hoccarihuay

That thou mayst raise me once more.

Yanayquin cani ccahuariy

Behold I am thy servant:

Cayqui quesayquita uyariy !

And so shall I ever be

(*Ccatisccaiquin y conanri*)

Ccoyllurniquita ccorihuay   If thou wilt grant me the
                                   Coyllur.

Chay ccanchayhuan purispa   Marching with that light
Ccan Apuyta yupaychaspa   I shall worship thee as Lord,
Huiñaytacc ccanta ccahuaspa   And for ever shall I praise thee
Huañunaypacc taquirispa.   Until the day of death.

YNCA PACHACUTEC.

Ollantay ccan runan canqui   Ollanta, thou art a man.
Hinallapitacc quepariy   Remain as thou art.
Pin casccayquita ccahuariy   Remember what thou hast been.
Ancha huichaytan ccahuanqui.   Thou lookest too high.

OLLANTA.

Huc camallaña sipihuay.   Take my life at once.

YNCA PACHACUTEC.

Ñoccan chaitacca ricunay   It is for me to see to that,
Manan ccampa acllanayquichu   It is not for thee to choose.
[Ñihuay Yuyayñiquipichu [39 a]   Dost thou know thyself?
Carccanqui? utccay ripullay.]   Go forth from my presence.
                                                      [*Exit.*
OLLANTA.

Ah Ollantay! Ollantay!   Ah Ollanta! Ollanta! [39 b]
Chainatachu hurccusunqui   Thus art thou answered
Llipi llactac cañiquiman   Thou who hast conquered.
Chai chica yanasccayquiman   Thou who hast served so well.
Ah! Cusi Ccoyllur huarmillay   Ah! Cusi Coyllur, my wife!
Cunanmi chincharichiqui   Now art thou lost for ever!
Ñan ñoca pisipachiqui   Thou art no longer for me!

Ay Ñusta! Ay Urpillay!	Ah Princess! Ah my dove!
Ay Cuzco! Ay sumac llacta!	O Cuzco! beautiful city!
Cunanmanta ccayamanca	From henceforth
Auccan casac, casac aucca	I will be thy enemy! thy enemy!
Chay ccasccoyquita ccaracta	I will break thy bosom without mercy,
Lliquirccospa sonccoyquita	I will tear out thy heart.
Cunturcunaman cconaypac	I will give thee to the condors!
Chay aucca! Chay Yncayquita!	That enemy! That Ynca!
Huñu huñu huaranccata	Millions of thousands
Anticunata [40] llullaspa	Of Antis [40] will I collect.
Suyuycunata tocllaspa	I will distribute arms,
Pusamusac pullccancata	I will guide them to the spot.
Sacsahuamanpin [41] ricunqui	Thou shalt see the Sacsahuaman [41]
Rimayta phuyuta hina	As a speaking cloud.
Yahuarpin chaypi puñunqui	Thou shalt sleep in blood.
Chaquiypin cancca Yncayqui	Thou, O Ynca! shalt be at my feet,
Chaypachan paypas ricuncca	Then shalt thou see
Pisinchus ñocapac Yunca	If I have few Yuncas.
Puchunccachus chay cuncayqui	If thy neck cannot be reached.
Manapunin ccoyquimanchu	Wilt thou not give
Ñihuanracc chay ususinta?	Thy daughter to me?
Pascarinracc chay siminta	Wilt thou loosen that mouth?
Manan ccampacca canmanchu	Art thou then so mad
Ñispa uticuy phinascca	That thou canst not speak,
Cconcor sayaspa mañactiy?	Even when I am on my knee?

D

Yncan paypas ñoca cacctiy

Tucuimi chaicca yachasca

Cunancca cayllaña cachun.

But I shall then be Ynca!

Then thou shalt know,

And this shall soon happen.

Enter PIQUI CHAQUI.

OLLANTA.

Piqui Chaqi puriy riy

Cusi Coyllur ñiyta niy

Cunan tuta suyahuachun.

Go, Piqui Chaqui,

Say to Cusi Coyllur

This night I await her.

PIQUI CHAQUI.

Ñacca rini, chisi rini

Cusi Coyllurpa huasinta

Tarini tucuyta chuita

Tucuytañan tapurini

Yesterday, late, I went

To the house of Cusi Coyllur;

I asked and no one answered—

There was not even a dog to be

seen,

Manan allcollapas canchu

(*misi*) [42]

Tucuy puncun huascarcosca [43]

Manañan pipas tianchu.

I could not find her—

All the doors were closed,

Nothing was to be seen.

OLLANTA.

Huarmancunari?

And her servants?

PIQUI CHAQUI.

Hucuchapas ayquepuscan

Manan micuyta tarispa

Tucu llañan sayarispa

Huc huacayta taquicuscan

(*Manchaitaña*).

Even the rats had gone,

Finding nothing to eat;

The owls only remained,

With their doleful music.

OLLANTA.

Yayanchari pusacapun	Perhaps her father has taken her,
Hatun huasinman pacarcoc.	To hide her in the palace.

PIQUI CHAQUI.

Ychapas payta huarcorcoc	Who knows if he has hanged her,
Mamantinmi pay chincapun.	And has abandoned her to the mother.

OLLANTA.

Mamachu pi ñocamanta	No one had asked
Tapuricun ccaynamanta.	For me yesterday ?

PIQUI CHAQUI.

Huarancca runallan ccanta	About a thousand men
Mascasunqui chaupichantin.	Seek to secure thee.

OLLANTA.

Tucuy suyu hatarichun	Then I will raise my province.
Tucuytan ttactanca maquiy	My hand shall destroy all.
Cay maccanan maquiy chaquiy	My hands and feet are my *macana.*[k]
Tucuytan champiycca ychun.	My club shall deal havoc.

PIQUI CHAQUI.

Ñocapas chay runataca	I too must trample
Haytaymanmi ccarataca	Upon this man.

OLLANTA.

Pi runata ?	What man ?

PIQUI CHAQUI.

Chay Urco-huaranccata ñini	I say that Urco-huarancca
Payllan canmanta tapucun.	He only has asked for thee.[1]

OLLANTA.

Yncas icha mascachihuan	Perhaps it is to say that the Ynca
Ñispan phiñacuscarcani.	Seeks me in his fury.

PIQUI CHAQUI.

Urco-huarancca, manan Ynca-chu	Urco-huarancca, not the Ynca.
Runallan chayni millacuy.	I abominate that little man.

OLLANTA.

Chincariñan Cuzcomanta	That he has fled from Cuzco
Cay sonccoymi huatupacun	My heart tells me,
Chay tucu chaytan huillacun	And the owl declares it.
[Ñac ripusun caymanta].	I will go with him.

PIQUI CHAQUI.

Ccoyllurtari saquesunchu.	We will leave the Coyllur.

OLLANTA.

Ymanasactac chincaptin !	How can I bear to lose her !
Ay Ccoyllur ! Ay Urpillay !	Ah Coyllur ! Ah my dove !

PIQUI CHAQUI.

Chay yarahuita uyariy	Listen to that *yarahui.*
Picha taquicun.	Who is it that sings !
	[*Music is heard within.*

SONG.

Urpi uyhuaytan chincachicuni	I lost a dove that I had cherished,
Huc chimlliyllapi !	In one moment !
Pacta ricuhuac mascariy puni (*tapucui*)	I searched for her in all parts,
Chay quitillapi.	Looking all round.
Millay munaymi sumac uyanpi	From the beautiful face of my love,
Ccoyllur sutinmi	They call her Coyllur.
Pacta pantahuac hucpa ccayllanpi	It was by reason of her beauty,
Ricuy sutinmi.	A harmonious name.
Quillahuan cusca [ynti] mattinpi	Like the moon in its splendour
Nanac capchiypi	Is her bright forehead,
Cuscan illancu hucpa sutimpi	When it shines in brilliancy
Ancha cusipi	In the highest heaven.
Ususi chucchanri chillu cayñinpi (*Llampu*)	Her sister tresses hang down,
Misatan ahuan	Woven in two colours,
Yanaquelluhuan llumpac rinripi (*yurachuan*)	Black mixed with gold upon her temples,
Ricuytan racran (*Nanacctan*)	A beautiful sight.
Quechip ñacuna munay uyampi (*rancuna*)	Her lovely eyebrows shading her face
Cuychin paccarin	Are like the rainbow.

Yscaymi Yntiquiquin ñahuimpi
    Chaymi sayarin
Quechiprallanri ñac chascca
    huachin (*nacai ccahuachin*)
    Tucuy sipicmi
Chaypin munaypas llipipac
    capchin
    Soncco siquicmi.

Her eyes are like two suns
    Fixed in her face.
Her penetrating glances

    Cause joy or sorrow ;
And though she is beloved and
    adored
    The heart is wounded.

Achancaraypas sisan uyampi

    Rittihuan cusca
Milluriyunacta sani utccapi
(*Mitun yuracpi*)
    Hinan ricuscca
Sumac simimpi ccantacmi
    pascan
    Rith piñita
Asispan ccapan misqui samas-
    ccan (*cconton*)
    Tucy quitita
    (*Tutui quiti*).

The *Achancaray* blooms on her
    cheek [44]
    Like snow ;
White as it appears upon the
    ground,
    So it is seen.
Her beautiful mouth is a sight

    Which rejoices the heart :
With the echo of her delicious
    laugh
    A joy is spread.

Llampi cuncanri quespi
    huayuscca
    Paraccay ritin
Utcu munaymi ccasconhuan
    cusca
    Huattan puririn

Her graceful throat is like
    crystal,
    Or driven snow ;
Her bosom increases from year
    to year,
    As growing cotton ;

Qqueque maquinri llullu cay- manpi	Her fingers are like icicles :
Cullarimpunin	As I gazed,
Rucanancuna ttacca cuyñinpi (*pascacuiñinpi*)	And as she moved them
Chulluncuy cutin.	They gave me joy.

OLLANTA.

Ay Cusi Coyllur!	Ah, Cusi Coyllur!
Ricsirccanchus cay taquicca	I recognize that music,
Sumayñiquita!	For it describes her beauty ;
Ripullachun cay llaquicca	The sorrow it brings back
Maytapas quita*	Remains with me.
Ñocan ccanta chincachiqui	If I should lose thee,
Muspallasacña	I shall go mad ;
Ñocan ccanta sipichiqui	If I should be deprived of thee,
Huañullasacña.	I shall die.

PIQUI CHAQUI.

Sipin punicha Ccoyllurta	Perhaps they have killed Coyllur,
Manan tutapas canchanchu.	Now the night is dark.

OLLANTA.

Ychacca ricsinccan Ynca	Perhaps the Ynca knows
Ollantaypa chusasccanta	That Ollanta is absent,
Tucuytan tarincca aucanta	That all are his enemies,
Tucuytacmi saquerencca.	And have abandoned him.

* All this omitted by Barranca.

PIQUI CHAQUI.

Hinantinmi munasunqui	You would want all
Ancha ccocucc cactiquicha	Because you are liberal.
Tucuypacmi raquicunqui	To all the world you are prodigal,
Ñocallapactacmi micha.	But to me you are penurious.

OLLANTA.

Ymapacmi can mananqui?	What would you have?

PIQUI CHAQUI.

Ymapac? chacpac, caipac	What! This, and this:
Sipasman ppacha cconoypac	To bestow clothing,
(*Hucman ppachata*)	
Huc collqueita ricunapac	To have plenty of silver,
Chayhuan manchanampac	And also to be feared.
(*Ñoccatari*).	

OLLANTA.

Phiña phiña puniyani	Be brave and valiant.
(*cai arï*)	
Chayhuan tucuy manchacusunqui.	With those you would be timid.

PIQUI CHAQUI.

Llachay mana chaypacchu	I have no taste for that;
(*Manan cai huyai*)	
Anchatan ñocca asini;	For I am always laughing,
Anchatatacmi casini;	I am always idle.
Qqueusuy manan ñoccapacchu.	Power is not for me.
(*Lercco cai*)	

Yma pututus huaccamun   What trumpet is that
   (*pitus*)
Carumantun caman hamun.   Sounding from afar?

OLLANTA.

Ñoccatachu mascahuancu   Perhaps they seek me.
Hacu ñaupariy.   Let us go.

PIQUI CHAQUI.

Ayquecpacca ñocan cani.   I am a fugitive.

                                    [*Exeunt.*

ACT II.

SCENE I.

Enter the Ynca Pachacutec, Rumi-Ñahui, *and Attendants.*

Ynca Pachacutec.

Ollantaytan mascachini	I ordered Ollantay to be sought for.
Mananpuniu tarincuchu (*paita*)	They have not yet found him.
Phiñayñiymi puchu puchu	My fury is great ;
Paypin llocllata [45] tarini	It bears me on like a torrent.
Ricunquichu chay runata ?	Hast thou seen that man ?

Rumi-Ñahui.

Manchariseeanc Ccapac ccancan (*campac*)	I have feared thee.
[Soncconpas chincariseeata	My heart is lost.
Ricuncani chay sallcata	I find a wilderness
Huchan punichari carccan].	In place of it.

Ynca Pachacutec.

Huarancca runata acllaspa	With a thousand chosen men,
Puriy payta mascamuhuay.	March in search of him.

Rumi-Ñahui.

Ñacha maytapas puririn	Where can he have gone
Quimsantin ppunchauñas chusan	In these three days,
Huasinmanta pichu pusan	That he has been away from his house ?
Chay raycun mana ricurin.	Why is he not found ?

Enter an Indian *with a quipu.*

Indian.

Cay quiputan apamuyqui	I bring you this *quipu*
Urupampamanta [46] cunan	From Urupampa,
[Huc chimlliypin ynti munan	They ordered me to come quickly.
Hamunayta ñan ricuyqui].	Now you have seen it.

Ynca Pachacutec.

Yman chaycunapi simi ?	What news are these ?

Indian. .

Chay quipucha huillasunqui.	That *quipu* will tell thee.

Brings a pole with coloured wool and grains of maize hanging from it.

Rumi-Ñahui.

Caycca llanta: ñan ccahuahuan	There is here a pole
Cay umanpi huatasccaña	To which a skein of wool is fastened :
Cay rurucunari runam	It reveals that there are as many men

Tucuy paymau tinquisccaña.   As grains of corn are here sus-
    (*huataccaña*)   pended.

YNCA PACHACUTEC.

Ymatan ccan ricurcanqui ?   What hast thou seen ?

INDIAN.

Ollantaytas tucuy Anti   The whole Anti nation
Runacuna chasquircancu   Has risen with Ollanta.
Hinatan huillacunccancu   It has been declared to me
Ccahuatas llautucun panti   That the red fringe was seen
Phurutas umallampi.   Encircling his brows.
(*O sanitac*)

RUMI-ÑAHUI.

Chaytan quipu huillasunqui.   This also the *quipu* says.

YNCA PACHACUTEC.

Amarac phiña tacyactiy   Before my fury abates
Puriy, puriy, can *huaminca*   March ! march ! O valiant war-
                          rior !

Callpayquiri pisicctinca   Go forth bravely
(Manarac ashuan chayactiy)   (Even with the force now here).
Pisca chunca huaranca   Fifty thousand men
Suyuquita tacurispa   Are raised in thy province.
Utccay utccay puririspa   March quickly ;
Muchuchinmi chayan.   The danger menaces.

RUMI-ÑAHUI.

Paccarillan llocsisacmi   I will go at once,
Huallahuisa yuparisccan   But now I had ordered
    (*camariscan*)

Ayqueccta hayccamusacmi
(*Ccollamañan puririscan*)
Cayman cutichimunapac
(*Tucuita harcamusacmi*)
Chay auccata sipinapac
Causactapas huañuctapas
Atisacmi runantapas
Ccanri Ynca! samariscay
[Huancunata camariscay].

Them to march to the land of
  the Collas,
All must be prepared

To capture this traitor,
Dead or alive.
This man shall submit
To thee, O Ynca! rest assured.
Be prepared for this.

[*Exeunt.*

SCENE II.

Enter OLLANTA, HANCO HUAYLLU, *and* URCO HUARANCCA,
with attendant Captains.

URCO HUARANCCA.

Ňan huamincca chasquisunqui
Anti-suyu runa-cuna :
Anchan huaccan huarmi-cuna
Ricunqui cunan ricunqui :
Chayantatas purincca
Tucuy runa, tucuy Auqui
Ancha carun purinayqui
Yma ppunchaucha taninca
Sapa huata llocsinanchis
Chay caru llactacunaman
[Chay aucca runacunaman]
Yahuartan llipi hichanchis

The valiant men receive thee,
Even the men of Anti-suyu ;
And the women also.
Thou shalt see! thou shalt see!
They will march to Anta.
All the men and their chief,
Thou shalt march with them.
May that day never come,
When every year they set out
For these distant villages,

To shed our blood,

Ñocanchispata paycunacta
(*Ña Yncacta ña paipata*)

Micuyñinta quespicuspan
As cucatari apacuspan
Purimuna llacta llacta
(*Saicuscancu tucui*)

Acco purunmi mascana
    (*rurunmi*)

Chaypin llamapas pisipan
Chaquitapas quiscattipan
(*Chaipin chaquinchista ttipan*)

Chaypin ccauchipi mitccana
(*Millai turpucpas quiscana*)

Unupas chaypacmi apana
Canumanta upyanapac
(*Huasancupi*)

Ñapecctuscca samanapac
(*Huañuitapas o suyana*)

(Huañuytahuanpashuaccyana).

To cut off from the Ynca

The provisions he needs.
By carrying a little coca
Every village will have rest.

It is needful to seek sandy ways;

And if the llamas become tired
We must walk on foot.

Although it be among thorns,

We must carry water
For drinking with us,

We must supply these things

To guard against death.

OLLANTA.

Apucuna uyariychis
Urcco Huarancca rimascanta

Chay saycuy sutinchascanta
    (*camariscanta*)
Sonccoyquichispi happiychis
Ccancunamanta llaquispan
(*Tucu Antila*)

Chiefs ! Listen
To the words of Urco Huar-
    ancca,

Saying you should rest ;

Preserve them in your memories,
Even when you are in mourn-
    ing.

Caracc Soncco ñini Yncata	I have the heart to tell the Ynca
Samarichun cunan huata	To desist during this year
Anti-suyu! sispan sispan	From invading Anti-suyu.
Chay runacunac ttocyanan	For his army would retreat
Sapa huatan llipillancu	In the year that comes,
Ña canascca ahuaranccu	Either from fatigue
Nanacc chuchucc onccoy manan	Or else from sickness,
(*Hina tocyan, hina onccocyan*)	
Chica caru purisccampi	Or from the long marches.
Maychica runan pisipan	The men would perish,
Maychica Auquin taripan	And many of the chiefs
Huañuyñinta ccaiccascampi	Would meet with death
Ccayta nispan llocsimun	In such an enterprize.
(*Hinan Anti*)	
Sapa Yncac ñauquinmanta	Thus would it be with the sole
(*Yncachispa*)	Ynca.
Manan ñinin hinamanta	If he should say no,
Ñoca cunam phahuamuni	I should fly to prevent him
Ama pipas llocsisunchu	From invading us.
Samaycuchis huasiquipi	Rest in your houses,
Noccatac llactayquichispi.	I shall be in your villages.
(*Ñoccan casac aucca chunchu*)	

ALL.

Yncaicu causay huiñaspac	May our Ynca live for ever!
Apu unanchacta hoccarey	Raise the great signal.
(*Puca*)	
Llautuyquipactac camariy	Prepare for him the llautu,
(*Sami chahuata achinaiquipac!*)	
[Puca ccahuata utccaypac]	And the crimson tunic.

Yncan paccarin tampupi

Let the Ynca appear in Tampu,

Yncan paccarin.   Yncan paccarin.

The Ynca is here!   The Ynca
is here!

Urco Huarancca.

Maquimanta chasquiy Ynca

O Ynca! receive in thy hands

Sayacc churascan llaututa

The crimson llautu we offer,

Caru carun Huillcañuta

How grand is Uillcañuta.

Huillca umuta huacyactinca

As Uillca are you seen

Hamullancan ppunchan tuta.

Day and night—the first among
us.[m]

They seat Ollanta *on the tiana, take off his yacollo,*[47] *and put
on him the royal robe and llautu.*

All.

Yncan paccarin Ollanta

Long live the Ynca Ollanta!

[Yncan paccarin.   Yncan paccarin.

Hail to the Ynca!   The Ynca!

Causapuasun.   Causapuasun.

Long may he live!   Long may
he live!

Llantuycausun.   Lllantuycau-
sun.

His life be our protection!

Soncontan chaypacc camarin

Our hearts are ready

Yayanchis hina uyhuaycausun

To obey our Father!

Churinta hina luluycausun

As a son he will love us,

Huac chancunata cuyaycausun

He will care for us,

Soncco ruranpi hatallihuasan.]

His heart will be ours.

[*The music plays, with tambors and pincullus.*

Ollanta.

Urcco Huarancca Auqui cay

Urcco Huarancca be noble!

Anti-suyuta camachiy

To rule over Anti-suyu!

Caycca chucuy, caycca huachiy	Here are these arrows, here this helmet !
Sinchi huaminccatac cay.	That you may also be valiant.

(*Huaminccaypas ccantac*) [Urco Huarancca *receives the arrows.*

ALL.

Urco Huarancca huaminca	O brave Urco Huarancca !
Causachun ! causachun !	Long may he live ! Long may he live !

OLLANTA.

Hancco huayllu : canmi canqui	Anco Huayllu as thou art
Ashuan yuyac hatun Auqui (*machu*)	A great and wise Auqui,
Ccanmi cunan churahuanqui	As thou art likewise
Huillac Umucc ayllun canqui (*Huillca*)	Of the lineage of the Uillac Umu,
Cay sipita huamincayman.	Put on these badges, and conquer death.

[*Puts on him the golden bracelet.*

HANCO HUAYLLU.

Huarancca cutin yupaychani	A thousand times, I venerate,
Ccapac Ynca rurascayquita.	O powerful Ynca, thy deeds.
Ccari ccarita ccahuariy	Behold the mighty warrior,
Umanmanta saphicama	From head to foot
Quiscahuan ppachallisccata	Bristling with arms.
Chaynan cana ccari ccari.	Surely he indeed is a warrior !
Maman hayccac ricunchu	Will he not behold
Huasayquita auccacuna ? (*auccaiquicuna*)	The backs of his enemies ?

E

Ayquehuactac Puna-runa [48]	He will neither fly like a moun-taineer
Manchahuactac llullu ccachu.[49]	Nor be humble as the weeds.

URCO HUARANCCA.

Uyariychis Anti-cuna	Choose, O men of Anti-suyu !
Ñan Yncanchis cunanccaña	What the Ynca advises.
Llapa runam tacyanaña.	All men take up arms—
(*Ñan cunancca yuyanaña*)	
Huñurañan suyucuna	All the provinces together.
(*Tacyananchis runa-cuna*)	
Machu Yncan Ccozcomanta	The old Ynca from Cuzco
Maccanata camarispa	To prepare their clubs,
(*Suyucunata*)	
Runantatacc tacurispa	And arouse their men,
(*Auquicunacta samispa*)	
Masca huasan quiquinmanta	Likewise it is his order.
(*Horccomunca maccanata*)	
Tucuy Ccozco lloccimuñan	All Cuzco will go forth
Cay huayccoman ñocanchista	To attack our lands
Sipinanpacc huasinchista	And destroy our houses,
Cananiytas aucca munan	Treating us as enemies.
(*Camareytan chaita munan*)	
Manan ppunchau usunanchu	Lose not a day,
Cay Orccocunapi masttariy	Prepare upon the hills
Ccompi-cunata camariy	The means of defence,
Manapunin ccasinachu	Let there be no waste of time.
tamputa paccay llutay	Quickly bar the quarters,

Huc puncullata haquespa	And leave one door open
(*s*)	
Tucuy Antini cheqquespa	Towards the Andes.
(*Orccocunapi hatarihuay*)	
Llapa onccopi hatariychis	Arouse all men at once
(*Hinantimpi miyuta cutay*)	
[Asca miyuta [50] cutaychis]	To grind all the poison
Huachinchista hampinapacc	And prepare our arrows,
Auccanchista sipirapacc	That in wounding the enemies
(*Chaihuan huachippitinanpacc*)	
Cay tucuytani utccaychis	Death may come at once.
(*Huañunampacc utccay utccay*).	

OLLANTA.

Urco Huarancca ccan acllascay	I have chosen thee, O Urco Huarancca !
Auquicunata ñaupacpac	First among the nobles :
Ayllu Aylluta pusacpac	To honour thy lineage.
(*vacapac*)	
Sayanantari unanchascay	I have marked thee to be alert.
Auccanchis manan puñunchu	Our enemies do not sleep.
Huc cutipi atipaspacca	Thou canst conquer them,
(*yaicuita*)	
Cutipunccan tacca tacca.	And force them to retreat.
Runa-cuna ccompisunchu.	Shall men not act as men ?

URCO HUARANCCA.

Ñan quimsa chunca huarancca	Here are thirty thousand
Anticuna cay [tampupi]	Antis in the *tampu—*
(*pi*)	

Manan ñocachis ucupi
Canchu quella canchu hancca.
Apu Maruti llocsincca
Uillca-pampa Anti-cunahuan
Chay ttinqui Queru[51] pataman
Chaypim happinca ruuanta
Pacascata huillanaycama
Llapan hatun soncco cama
(*Chimpanpitacmi hinatacc*)
Auqui Chara runantatacc
Pacancca huac yanaycama
Chara munaypim puñuncca
Chunca huarancca Antinchis
Pacharpi[52] Camayoc ñinchis
(*Pachar huaiccopin hapinchis*)
Huc chuncattatac Ayllunca
Yaycumuchun Cozcocuna
Upallaspalla Suyusun
(*Ama rimarispa suyai*)
Tucuy toellapi cacctinri
      (*ucupi*)
Lluttasccan puncunchiscuna
(*Quirpasccan*)
Huateccaspalla Suyusun
(*Lloellamunccan munay munay*)
Putucunchista phucuna
Chay pachañan Orccocuna
Chapicunca rumintinri
Chuchin urmamuncca rumi

Amongst us all
There is neither coward nor sick.
The Chief Maruti will go forth
With the Antis of Uilca-pampa,
To the confluence of the Queru,
Where he shall conceal his men
Until I give the order.
All have large hearts.

The noble Chara with his men
Shall wait on the other bank.
There shall sleep with Chara
Ten thousand Antis.
In the valley of Pachar

Shall be other ten *Ayllus*.
Until the Cozcos enter
We will quietly wait.

When all are within

We will close the entrance,

And it shall be as a flood.

At the the sound of the conch
The rocky hills
Shall pour out stones,
The stones shall be as hail.

Huanccacunan huicupancca	The missiles shall roll down,
Tucuyta chaypin ppampanca	All shall be buried,
Chaymi paicunapac tumi	This will be their punishment.
Chaypachan ayqquccunacca	As for the fugitives
Maquinchispi huañunccacu	They will die by our hands,
Quespiy attic huaquincuna '	Or by the poison of our arrows.
(*Huachinchispin*)	
Tturpuscca ricurinccacu.	

[*They play pincullus and pututas, and exeunt, shouting:—*	[*They play flutes and conches, and exeunt, shouting :—*

ALL.

Allinmi! Allinmi!	Good! Good!

————

SCENE III.

Enter RUMI-ÑAHUI *dressed in mourning, with two Attendants.*

RUMI-ÑAHUI.

Sallocc Rumi! Rumi Ñahui!	Ah Rumi! Rumi Ñahui!
Yma quencha rumin canqui	What an unfortunate art thou!
Ccaccamantan llocsircanqui	Thou hast escaped from a rock—
Sonccoyquim curaca ccahuy!	For me it is a sad yarahui!
(*Chaimi ccasapac Yarahui*)	
Manachu maquiqui carccan?	Have you not in your hands,
Chay huayccopi pacasccata	Hidden in this valley,
Ollantayta ccarcoscata	The fugitive Ollanta?
Manachu yuyarircanqui	Dost thou not remember
Tapara soncco casccanta?	That he has a treacherous heart?

Tucuy macanacusccanta ?	With all his arms
Manachu ccan ttactarcanqui ?	Shalt thou not pull him down?
Hinantimpi llullacuspa	Why hast thou not tried
Sayucunata ichurcca	The arts of stratagem
Payllapipunin tincurccan	To deceive his army?
Qquello cay ccari tucuspa?	He, being weak, has become valiant.
Chica huarancca runata	A thousand men
Cunan ppunchau sipichini	In this day
Ñocca ñaccayta qquespini	I have slain
Maquinmanta : chay ccanata	With this hand.　Thus only
Ñoccaca ccaricha ñispa	I escaped.　They thought
Uyapura mascarccani	That he was a coward,
Chay huayccoman yaycurccani	Therefore I sought him,
Ayqquenpunim chaycca ñispa	Thinking he would fly.
Na suyuy puncumpi caspa	But in the entrance of his camp,
Urmamuyta ccallarimun	On every side,
Tucuy ccacca ppucchirimun	Rocks began to fall,
Huanccacunata huaccyaspa	Bringing with them many blows.
Hinantimpin rumi ñitin	Thus the volleys of stones,
Hinantimpin ccacca pacan	And the many rocks,
Ashuan acllascacunatan	Killed and buried my men.
Chaypi caypi cumpa sipin	Here and there they fell,
Yahuarllan tucuy huayccopi	The blood ran in the valley,
Parin llocllan masttaricun	Flowing like a torrent.
Hinantinmi chayta ricun	I also beheld
Ñoccapas yahuar pponccopi	A quantity of blood;
Pihuantacc tincuyman carccan	Yet I saw no one,
Mana runan llocsimuctin	No man came forth,

Mana pipas ricurictin	None could be seen,
Huancca cuna huarcca huarc-can	But my men were killed.
Yma uyahuan tincusacc	How can I return
Yncahuan cunan ccayllampi	To appear before the Ynca?
Manan canchu caypacc hampi.	I indeed am lost !
Risac maytapas ripusac	Whither shall I fly ?
Ñan cunan seccocuymaña	I will hang myself
Cay huaracahuan ñoccallata	With my own sling.
Ycha cachus pay camalla	The same will serve,
Ollantaypas urmanccaña.	When Ollanta shall fall.
(*haicac*)	[*Exit.*

SCENE IV.

Enter Yma Sumac *and* Pitu Salla.

Pitu Salla.

Ama chicata puncuman	Yma Sumac, do not go
Yma Sumac llocsillaychu	To the door so often.
Amatacc chaypi suyaychu	Do not wait there,
Mamacunam phiña cunam.	Lest the matrons be vexed ;
Yma Sumac sutiquipas	Thy name is Yma Sumac,
Ancha munacusccay ñaña	And it is well beloved.
Hinapitacc pay camaña	Only to hear it
Huillapunman maypas pipas	And to pronounce it
Acllaman [53] cusita cconam	The Virgins are filled with joy.
Cay canchapi huesccacuspa	When thou art here
Tiyay caypi cusicuspa	Thou art surrounded with pleasure.

Pin caymanta pita horcconan	No one ever goes out.
Caypin taricunqui ricuy	Here thou shalt see
Tucuy yma ccoñiquita	All kinds of comforts—
Sumac ppachata ccorita	Beautiful cloth of gold,
Caypin tucuy misqui micuy	And sweet food.
Ynca yahuar acllacuna	The Virgins of Ynca blood
Llapallanmi munasunqui	Love thee, all of them,
Tucuyllancu yuyacc cunac	All the mistresses
(*Tucuy tucuy*)	
(*Maquincupin apasunqui*)	
Ña muchaspa ña llulluspa	Kiss and are fond of thee.
Ccasconcupi churasunqui	Thee alone they set apart,
Ccanllatan huayllusunqui	Thee only they love
(*acllacu*)	
Uyayquipi ccahuacuspa	And embrace.
Ymatan ashuan munanqui?	What more canst thou want?
Huc ñañancu canayquipac	Thou who shouldst serve the sisters,
Paycunahuan tiyanayquipac	Sit down with them all.
Chaytan ccampas unanchanqui	Thou shouldst also know
Tucuy Auquip yupaychasccan	That thou art accounted noble,
Ynca yahuar acllacaman	And as a royal virgin.
(*Yma*)	
Yntita ccahuaspa saman	Thou art as a child of the sun,
Ynticc hallanpac camascan.	They guard thee, as belonging
(*Ttallampac*)	to the sun.

YMA SUMAC.

Pitu Salla, millay cutin	Pitu Salla, many times,
Chayllatacc, chayllatatacc	Only this, only this,

Cunahuanqui ñoccaracctacc	You say to me.
Rimarisacc chaymi sutin	Now I will speak
Anchatan checnipacuni	The very truth.
Cay canchata cay huasita	This court, this house,
Caypi caspa cay ccasita	The useless life,
Ppunchau tuta ñacacuni.	Days and nights I hate.
(ppunchau)	
Cay payacunacc uyanta	The faces of the old women
Ancha aputa ccahuascani	Above all I detest.
Payllatatacc ricuscani	That is all I can see
Chay ccuchu tiascaymanta	From the corner where I sit.
Manan cusi caypi canchu	In this place there is no joy,
Hueqquen uyancupi caicca	Only tears to weep.
Munaiñimpi canman chaicca	Your wish would be
Manan pipas tianmanchu	That none should live here.
Ccahuani puriccunata	They all walk, as I see,
Asicuspan ccuchicuncu	Between laughing and crying,
Maquincupi apacuncu.	Their fate in their hands,
Llipipas samincunata	Full of anxiety.
Ñoccallachu huisccacusac	I am shut up here,
Mana Mamay casccan raycu?	Because I have no mother.
Ccapac ttalla canay raycu	Having no good nurse to tend me,
Cunanmanta qquesacusacc	I have been to seek for one.
Huc tutan mana puñuspa	Last night I could not sleep,
(Caina tutan muspha muspha)	
Muyanchisman yaycurcani	I wandered to the garden,
Hinaspan uyarircani	And there I heard,
(Hinapin)	
Chica chimpi ricucuspa	In the moment I was there,

Haccacuyta pis ñacarin	A voice of mourning,
Chica llaqui cuyapacuspa	Groans and cries of one
Huañullayman ñin ccaparin	Who prayed for death.
Hinantintan ccahuarini	I looked all round,
Chucchaypas chascallicuspa	With hair dishevelled,
Huacyani mancharicuspa	Who art thou that mourns
Pipas cay riccuniy ñini.	So sadly ? I exclaimed.
Yapatacmi ccaparimun	Take me from hence,
Yntillay horccohuay-ñispa	O sun ! deliver me.
Ancha cuyayta anchispa	I looked all round ;
Soncco qquehuiyta hiqquiman	My heart trembled.
(*Yapa yapapai*)	
Chaccayta caytan mascani	I searched but in vain,
Mana pita tarinichu	I found nothing,
Huayallapi chihuin ychu	Only the grass whistling in the meadow.
Ñoccari pay huahua cani	I am but a child ;
(*paihuan huaccani*)	
Soncccoytacc lliquicuspa	My heart almost
Ccascoyta saqqueyta munan	Leapt from my bosom.
Yuyarini choypas cunan	Even now, when I remember,
Mancharinin sipicuspa	I am full of terror.
Hinan caypi Pitu-Salla	Even now, Pitu-Salla,
Llaquillan quiquin quesacun	The same sorrow haunts me ;
Huiqquellan huiñay sisacun	And the grief lasts for ever.
Yachay hinan munay ttalla	O my beloved nurse,
Amapuni cunanmanta	Listen to my wish.
Rimanquichu qquepanayta	Do not say I am to stay ;
Checninim cay acllanayta.	I hate this state of seclusion.

PITU SALLA.

Yaycupuy ari ucuman	Go in. Do not let
Pacta paya llocsimunman.	Any of the old women see you.

YMA SUMAC.

Cay ccanchan ñoccapacmi ?	Is this place for me ?

Enter COACCA MAMA, *dressed entirely in white.*

CCACCA MAMA.

Pitu Salla ñirccanquichu	Pitu Salla, hast thou given
Chay herqqueman cunasccaita?	My orders to this child ?

PITU SALLA.

Ymaymantam huillani ?	What should I tell her ?

COACCA MAMA.

Yma ñintacc simiquiman.	What I have told you.

PITU SALLA.

Ancha cuyaitan huaccacun	She weeps without ceasing,
Manapunin uyacunchu	And will not put on
Aclla ppachata chasquicuyta.	The dress of the virgins.

CCACCA MAMA.

Manacha anyarircanqui ?	Hast thou not censured her ?

PITU SALLA.

Pachatan ccahuarichini	I showed her the dress,
Huaccha cascanta horccospa	That she might take off
Ña huamanmanta ccarcospa	The old clothes she wears.
Chay yuyayta hinan ñini	I tell her she is not a child ;

Mana aclla canqui chayca.	And that she cannot be a chosen one :
Millay llaquin ccatisunqui	That, being dirty and sad,
[Yanapacun ccan muyunqui	She must be a servant
Cay huasipi ñispa laycca.]	Always in this house.

CCACCA MAMA. (To YMA SUMAC).

[Munancca, Mama, munancca	For thy loving nurse
Cay ppachatan pay chasquircca	Wilt thou not change thy clothes ?
Mana chairi pay ricuncca]	Seest thou not this dress ?
Ppasñallan huiñaypac canqui	Thou shalt always be a servant;
Ymapaccha pay yuyacun	Thou shalt know thy dress ;
Usuri mana yayayocc	A daughter without a father,
Huillullu mana mamayocc	A child with no mother.
(Uc herqque)	
Chaccay pucac taparacum.⁵⁴	Here is a large butterfly (a bad omen),
Sutinta ñinqui sutinta	Say thy name, thy name.
Chaypacc canqui caycunapi	Thou art here shut up,
(Canmi cai percacunapi)	
Tucuy pacac accarapi	Closed up within these walls,
Tucuy milpucc sutintinta.	And even thy name is forgotten.
	[Exit.

PITU SALLA.

Ay Yma Sumac ! Yma Sumac !	Oh, Yma Sumac ! Yma Sumac !
Pacanmanchas uyayquita	Thou wilt be concealed.
Yma percca sapayquita	What wall will hide you, in solitude,

Accoy ñircacc casacc pumacc !⁵⁵   Here a serpent, there a lion ?

(*Caicca Amaru caicca puma*)   [*Exeunt.*

SCENE V.

Enter Rumi-Ñahui * *on one side, and* Piqui Chaqui *on the other, looking about very carefully. They see each other.*

Rumi-Ñahui.

Maymantatac Piqui Chaqui   Whence, Piqui Chaqui,

(*Yma hinan ccan*)

Cayman ccancca chayamunqui   Dost thou come?

Huañuytachu masccarcanqui   Dost thou seek death

Aucca Ollantayhuan huaqui ?   With the traitor Ollanta ?

(*Ollantayhuan cusca*)

Piqui Chaqui.

Ccosco-runa caspan huichu   Being a native of Cuzco,

Llactallaiman hampucuni   I come to my town

Chay huayccopi manapuni   In yonder ravine,

Yachacuyta atinichu.   I can no longer stay.

Rumi-Ñahui.

Ymatan Ollantay ruran ?   What is Ollanta doing ?

Piqui Chaqui.

Chay ccaytutan cururan   I am spinning this heap of wool.

    (*quipucta*)

Rumi-Ñahui.

Yma ccaytu ? yma cururta ?   What heap ? what wool ?

---

* Von Tschudi has Huillca Uma.

PIQUI CHAQUI.

Tapuhuaycca ccoycunaspa   Dost thou ask me?   Give me
(*Ymatapas cunan ccohuai*)
Chay pachacca huillascayqui.   Those clothes, and I will tell.

RUMI-ÑAHUI.

Huc allin caspita huatanaypacc   I will give you a good stick,
Quimsatatacc huarcunaypacc.   And to hang you—three.

PIQUI CHAQUI.

Ama manchachicu huaychu.   Oh, do not frighten me.

RUMI-ÑAHUI.

Utecayta rimariy ari.   Then speak quickly.

PIQUI CHAQUI.

[Ccanpas uyarihuay ari   But you will not listen.
Ñoccacca ñausay apuniu   I am turning blind,
Rimriypas upayapunmi   My ears are getting deaf;
Machulaycca huañupumi   My grandmother is dead,
Mamaytacca cconccapunmi.   And my mother is alone.

RUMI-ÑAHUI.

[Maipin ñinay Ollantaycca?   Where is Ollanta?   Tell me!

PIQUI CHAQUI.

[Chusapunaccanmi tataycca   My father is from home,
Manan pocconchu paccayca   And the paccays are not ripe.
Pocchupurccanmi callpayca   I have a long walk to-day,
Sasan chay cuncu llantaycca   It is difficult to carry me.
Ynca uccupin Mancanaycca   The Ynca would cut up his
                                   body.

Ancha carus sallccantaycca].   The desert is very far off.

Rumi-Ñahui.

[Astahuan phiñachihuascay If you vex me again
Ricuyhuancunccoyquimantacc.] I will take your life.

Piqui Chaqui.

Ollanta? ccanin sayarin.	Ollanta? He is at work.
Ollanta? pircata hoccarin	Ollanta? He raises a wall
Ancha huanccacc rumimanta.	Of very great stones,
Hina runacunamanta	With his men.
Yscayta hucman huatarin	He fastens two dwarfs,
Hatun runa llocsinanpacc	That a giant may come forth.
Ymanasccan ccan Yncacri	Tell me! why are you,
Umpu ancac hina surun	Like the eagle spreading his
(*huallpa*)	wings,
Cay ppachayqui ricuy tturun	With such long clothes,
Qquellichacunmi yanari.	That the mud stains black?

Rumi-Ñahui.

Manachu Ccosco llactata	Seest thou not the city of Cuzco
Ccahuarinqui huaccascacta	Is filled with mourning,
Pachacutec pampascata	Pachacutec is buried—
Ricullay llapa runata	All men are dressed
(*llata*)	
Tucuymi yanata pachan	In mourning clothes,
Tucuymi hueqquecta huaccan.	And there is great lamentation?

Piqui Chaqui.

Pitac Ynca tiay cuncca	Who shall be Ynca
(*cunanri sayanca*)	
Pachacutec rantintani?	To succeed Pachacutec?
(*qquepantari ?*)	

Rumi-Ñahui.

Ccapac Yupanqui sayancca.   Ccapac Yupanqui stands.

(*Thupac*)

Piqui Chaqui.

[Pachacutec churillanca]   Though Pachacutec has sons
Qqueparinccan asccatacmi   In great number,
          (*punin*)
Cacctacmi huc cunac llancca?   Shall it still be him?

Rumi-Ñahui.

Tucuy Cozcon acllan payta   All Cuzco has declared it.
Yncari llauttuntan saqquen   The Ynca has assumed the *llautu*,
Champintan saqquen camaq-   He has taken the *champi*.
          quen
Atincuchu hucta acllaita   Him alone can we choose,
[Ccanmi ccatihuay utccayta.]   He alone can be taken.

Piqui Chaqui.

Apamusac puñunayta.   I must go to fetch my bed.

                                        [*Exit.*

SCENE VI.

Enter Ccapac Yupanqui, *the* Uillac Umu, *and* Nustas,
(*Thupac*)   *with attendants.*

Yupanqui.

Cunan ppunchaumi Auqui-cuna   On this day, O nobles!
Llapata yupaychayquichis   All of you should worship
Yntiman chasquichiquichis   And venerate the sun.
Yntic huarmin caccunan   All virgins that exist

Hinantin suyun cusicun
Cay canchaypi ricuspa
Sonccoy hinatac yupaspa
Ccancunata yuyan ricun.

Are filled with joy,
To see it in this place.
Remember your duty,
To pray with your hearts.

Uillac Umu.

Ccayna ppunchau saya ccosñin
Yntic suyun uyancama
Chasquincancha Pachacamac
Tucuy ccanam sami llocsin
Hucllan Ynca tacurirccan

Yesterday the smoke arose
To the region of the Sun.
Pachacamac is now
Filled with joy.
But one thing has moved the Ynca—

Piscocuna canasccapi
Llamacuna rupasccapi
Tucuy runan ccahuarinccan
Huc ancatan quicharccaicu
Ccasconta ccahuaicunapac
Sonccomanta recsinapac
Chusacllatan tarircaycu
Chay ancan Antinsuyuyqui
Utccay chaita huñupuna
Ccasacunmi y chaicuna
Chaitan cunan huatupuyqui.

In the sacrifice of birds,[56]
In the burning of llamas,
All men have seen.
We opened an eagle
To observe his bosom,
And divine from his heart.
We found it empty.
That eagle, as to Anti-suyu,
Shows we shall soon
Put down the revolt—
It augurs that they will submit.

Ccapac Yupanqui.

Cay Anansuyu Huaminccan
Chay Ancata quespichirccan
Payllatac chincarichirccan
Chay chicca runacunata.

That valiant Anansuyu
Left this eagle free—
And she has been the destruction
Of so many men.

F

Rumi-Ñahui.

Ñan Apu Ynca Yuyayqui	Great Ynca, thou knowest
Hunttasccataña yacharccan	All that has happened,
Chaicca huchaypunin carccan	And what are my sins.
Rumincani cay camayqui	Although I am a stone,
Rumin ñittirccan tucuyta	I will obey thee as a stone.
Rumihuanmi llocsircani	I went forth with a stone,
Payhuan macana curcani	And with it I fought,
Chaymi atirccancu suyuita	Though they held the province.
Huc llatan mañacuscayqui	There is only one thing
Saqquehuascay ñoccallaman	That I would ask;
Noccan risac pucaranman	It is that I may go to the fortress ;
Llaquen ñocca aisamusccayqui.	I promise to gain a victory.

Ccapac Yupanqui.

Ccampan chaycca ruranayqui	Here is what thou must do
Chay sutiquita hoccaripuy	To recover thy name—
Mana chayri cacharipuy	Thou must not abandon
Suyuta : hinan camayqui.	The province. Such is thy duty.

Uillac Umu.

Pisi ppunchaupin ricunqui	Thou shalt see, in a few days,
Anti-Suyuta chaquiquipi	Anti-suyu at thy feet ;
Hinan tincuni quipuyquipi	So I find in the *quipus.*
Utccay utccay rumi tunqui.	Fly! Fly! Rumi-*tunqui.*[57]

[*Exeunt.*

[*A scene with Rumi-Ñahui and a Cañari Indian, not in my manuscript, is here inserted by Von Tschudi and Barranca. I believe it to be a modern interpolation.*]

SCENE VII.

Enter OLLANTA *and* RUMI-ÑAHUI *covered with blood.*[58]

RUMI-ÑAHUI.

Huarancca cutin muchani	A thousand times I adore,
Ccapac Ynca maquiquita	Powerful Ynca, thy hand.
(*yupiquita*)	
Cuyapayay huac chayquita	Have pity on this unfortunate;
[Chaqui quipitaccami cani].	I am at thy feet.

OLLANTA.

Pin canqui cayman purirei?	Who art thou? Whence dost thou come?
Pin chay hinata rurasunqui?	Who has done this to thee?—
Maiñecmanta musphamunqui	From whence hast thou fallen?
(*urma*)	
Chica usupa chica quiri.	Who has thus wounded thee?
(*Pitac canqui*)	

RUMI-ÑAHUI.

Anchatan can recsihuanqui	You know me well;
Rumin cani chay ccormani	I am that Rumi.
Chaquiquiman chaymi urmani	For this I have fallen at thy feet.[59]
Ccan Yucan horccarihuanqui!	O Ynca, favour me!

OLLANTA.

Sayarimui cay ricnayman	Rise. Here you have my hand.
(*maqueiman*)	
Pin chainata rurasunqui	Who has done this to you?

Pin cayman pusamusunqui   Who has led you

Cay tampu llacta casccayman   To my town, to my lodging?

    (*iman cai nauqueimani*)

Mosoc ppachata apamuy   Bring new clothes,

Munasccaimi cay Auquicca?   For I love this nobleman.

Ymanasccan sapayquicca,   Why art thou abandoned?

Manan canchu ccanpac huañuy.   Thou shalt not die.

Rumi-Ñahui.

Mosocc Yncan chay Cozcopi   The new Ynca, in Cuzco,

Ccapac Yupanqui tiyaicun   Tupac Yupanqui, is now en-

(*Tupac*)   throned.

Caymi Tucuyllata raycun   He is a cruel tyrant:

Causac yahuar phosoccopi   He lives in the midst of blood;

Hinantintiña ccorospa   He shows no mercy;

Manan sonccon tiyaycunchu   He never softens his heart;

Tucuy ñucchun puca sunchu   Like the red *ñucchu* and the

                      sunchu,[60]

Tucuyta sipin mosccospa.   He devours all in his madness.

Carccani : ychas yuyanqui   Perhaps you may remember me.

Chayta yachaspan Yupanqui   Knowing me, this Yupanqui

Huac yahuar paypa camanmi   Has drawn this blood.

Chay caracc soncco caiñimpi   In his depraved heart

Cayta ruray, cayta camay   He does one thing, and imagines
                      another.

Ñan ricunqui mama yayay   You are now father and mother
                      to me.

Caynam quiribuan huasinpi.   Here you have me in your
                      house.

OLLANTA.

Ama llaquichu Rumi	Do not be afflicted, Rumi,
Ñocca cunam hampisccayqui	I will now cure you,
Ccantatacmi cahuascayqui	I will give you help.
Ccanmi canqui paypac tumi	You also must prepare your knife;
Ynti huatana ppunchaupi	On the day of *Ynti-huatana*,
Cay tampupi hatun raymi	A great *Raymi*, in this tampu,
Chaypacha ccochucunaymi	Will be celebrated.[61]
Tucuypas ccochucamusun	Then we must advance
Pucarapi hayllimusun.	From the fortress, with songs.

RUMI-ÑAHUI.

Quimsa ppunchau raymi cachun	The *Raymi* will be for three days;
Cusicuypas tacsa canman	The time of joy is short;
Chaypacc ichas alliyaiman	By that time I shall be well.
Soncconco chaypac rimachun.	I speak from my heart.

OLLANTA.

Hinan cancca, quimsa tuta	So be it. Three nights,
Hatun Yntita huatasun	We gaze on the great Sun;
Cusipi tucuy tiasun	We shall be seated in joy,
Huisccasunchis cay tamputa.	For that time the *Tampu* is closed.

RUMI-ÑAHUI.

Huarmicunatan cunana	The servants shall be told
Paycunac tatanmi cancca	That they may arrange for the night.
Paycunan caypi samancca	Also they should bring
Huarmi ccasccanta apana.	Their women with them.

[Exeunt.

ACT III.

SCENE I.

Enter YMA SUMAC *and* PITU SALLA, *from opposite sides.*

YMA SUMAC.

Munacusccay Pitu Salla	Dearest Pitu Salla,
Haycac caman pacahuanqui	How long will you hide
Chay simita? Ricuy Salla	This from me? See, Pitu,
Cay sonccoytan patmihuanqui	How you have torn my heart
Caina hucqquehuan camalla	By not telling me yesterday,
(*Sipihuanquin huc*)	
Cayta upallahuaspayqui	Why are you so silent?
(*Mana can huillahuaspayqui*)	
Pithuiscanin huchaymanta	It may be for my sins
Picha llaquin caiñeccmanta.	That I desire to know.
Ama pacahuaichu urpi	My Dove! do not keep it from me:
Pitac phutin pitac huaccan	Who is it that mourns
Cay chiuñic muya ucupi?	Each instant, within the garden?
[Huillayculla huayna urpi.	Speak, my young Dove!
Mainiccpitac paita pacan	Why is it hidden from me?
Cay chica sumac suturpi?	Tell me, beautiful one.
Ñihuay pitac payta huarccan	She who thus makes her moan,
Ñoccaman ricurimanta	Why may I not see her—
Ñoccahuan rimaycunanta.] *	Why may I not speak to her?

* Von Tschudi has only two lines here.

Pitu Salla.

Yma Sumac huillasscayqui	Yma Sumac, I will tell
Huellata ccanmi ichacca	To you, what you would know;
Ymatapas ricuspayqui	But you must hide it,
Pacaycunqui rumi ccacca	As if thy bosom were a rock;
Ñan ccantacca ricuscayqui	For that which you will see
Ancha llaquitan ricunqui	Will cause you great sorrow,
Milluy cutin y phuyunqui.	And you will be without comfort.

Yma Sumac.

Manan piman huillasacchu	Do not conceal it,
Yma haycata ricuspapas	Do not hide anything :
Amapuni pacahuaychu	To no one will I confide it ;
Millpusacmi tucuytapas.	I know how to bury it.

Pitu Salla.

Cay muyapin ccacca puncu	Wait for me at the door
Cayllallapi suyacuhuay	Belonging to the garden,
Llipi Mama puñuchunca	When all the matrons sleep,
Ñan tutaña tiaycuscay.	In the dead of night.

[*Exit.*

Yma Sumac.

Ymaymantan yuyascan	What shall I then know !
Cay sonccoy huatupacuspa	My heart seems to guess.
Ricullayman pis huaccascan	How much shall I grieve
Cay penccapi hiquicuspa.	When it is shown to me !

Enter PITU SALLA, *with a light, a cup of water, and a small covered vase.*

PITU SALLA.

Hatarei cunan ccatahuay	Now is the time,
Cay canchata pacaycuspa.	Rise and cover the light.

Opens a door concealed in the wall, discovering a small room with CUSI COYLLUR *chained to the wall, senseless.*

Caymi Ñusta mascascayqui	Here is the hidden Princess.
Ñachu sonccoyqui taninña ?	Does thy heart cease to beat ?

YMA SUMAC.

Ay ñaña, ymatan ricuni !	Alas ! what do I see ?
Ayatachu pacanccanqui ?	Have you hidden a corpse here ?
	[*Faints.*

PITU SALLA.

Ymatac caycca ñoccapac	What has happened to me ?
Yma Sumac urpillay !	O Yma Sumac ! my Dove !
Cutinpuay cunanllapac	Return to thyself.
Hampuy, hampuy, Sicllallay.[62]	Get well ! get well ! my Siclla.

Throws a little water in her face, and YMA SUMAC *comes to herself, hiding behind* PITU SALLA.

Ama ñaña manchariychu	Do not fear, my sister,
Manan ayachu huc huaccha	She who weeps is not a corpse ;
Ñustan caypi llaquipacha.	It is a Princess who is here.

YMA SUMAC.

Causanrachu cay huarmicca?	Is that woman still alive?

PITU SALLA.

Asuycamuy yanapahuay	Come near and help me.
Causanracmi ricuy ccahuay	See! she is yet alive.
Hay huarihuay cay unuta	Bring me some water,
Mattiy cuytacc chay puncuta.	And shut well the door.

She throws a little water in CUSI COYLLUR's *face,*
who comes to herself.

Sumac Ñusta ymananmi	Beautiful Princess, wherefore thus?
Caycca unu, caycca micuy	Here is water, here is food.
Asllatahuan tiyaricuy	Rest thyself a little;
Cunallunmi yayamuni.	But now I must be gone.
(*Yaicumuni cunallanmi*)	

YMA SUMAC.

Pillan canqui sumac urpi	Who art thou? Beautiful Dove,
Asllatapas micunihuac	Will you not eat a little,
Ychas chayhuan causarihuac.	To keep thyself alive?

CUSI COYLLUR.

Yma ashuatan munascani	Here is what most I love.
Chica ascca huatamanta	After so many years,
Huc huahuata habuamanta	O my child! my child!
Yaycumucta ricuscani.	I see thee once more.

Yma Sumac.

Ay Ñustallay sumac halla	O beautiful Princess!
Sumac chayña [63] ccoriquitu (*pisco*)	Beautiful golden finch!
Ymapitac can camalla	What hast thou done?
Hucharcanqui urpita?	How hast thou sinned, my Dove?
Ymanasca chica calla	Why have they oppressed you?
Ymanasca canca pitu	Why have they made you suffer?
Cay huañuyhuan pittuiscanqui	Do you desire death,
Puytucc puncupiña canqui?	Thus shut and tied up?
(*Cai ccarihuan huanqui huan-qui.*)	

Cusi Coyllur.

Sumac huahua, munay ruru,	Lovely child! beloved fruit!
Ñoccaca huc huarmin cani	I am a woman,
Cay puytupi panti [64] muru:	Like the seed of the *panti*.
Ñoccan casaracurcani	I was married to one,
Huc ñaui ruruta hina	Who was as the apple of my eye.
Payri concca huareccan phiña	They married me to him
Manan yacharcanchu Ynca	Without the knowledge of the Ynca,
Payhuan huatasca casccayta	Who turned upon me
Hinapi Ollantay manactinca	And banished Ollanta.
Phiñacuspa ccarccon paita	Before, he was in favour.
Ñoccatari ripuctinca	As for me, I was sent
Camachin caypi camaita,	As a prisoner here.
Nanac huatan caypi cani	Now it is many years

Ricuy ymaynas causani
Mana ricunichu pita
Cay yana huatay huasipi

That I have lived in this place.
See how I am
In this prison, without a companion.

Manan ñoccapas samita
Tarinichu cay misquipi
Suyacunin chunca mitta
Huañunayta cay sipipi
Cay quellay huascahuan huatascca

Here there is no joy.
What pleasure can be here ?
Ten times I am ready
To welcome death,
Fastened with chains

Tucuypatac ni cconccasca
Canri pitac canqui lulu
Chica huarma chica llullu ?

And forgotten by all.
But who art thou,
So young and so tender ?

Yma Sumac.

Ñoccapas ccantan ccatiqui
Phuticuspa huccacuspa
Ususcanin cay huaspi

I have always sought thee,
Transported with grief:
From the time I was in this house

Sonccoimi ccanta ricuspa
Ccasucun cay ccascollaypi
Manan mamay yayaicanchu
Manan pipas riccsihuanchu.

My heart leapt within me
That I might know thee.
I have no father nor mother,
And know no one as such.

Cusi Coyllur.

Haica huatayocmi canqui ?   How old are you ?

Yma Sumac.

Millay huatayoccha cani
Cay huasita chiccnicuspa

Perhaps I have many years.
I hate this house,

Hinapaccmi yupasccani	And I have not counted
Mana caypi yachacuspa.	While I have lived here.

PITU SALLA.

Huc chunca hinacha huatan	She has about ten years,
Hinatan ñocca yupani.	So I count.

CUSI COYLLUR.

Yman ccampa sutinquicca?	What is your name?

YMA SUMAC.

Yma Sumac sutei carccan	They call me Yma Sumac.
Chaypas suteitan pactarccan.	But perhaps I am not like my name.

CUSI COYLLUR.

Ay huahua! Ay urpillay!	O my child! O my dove!
Cay ccascoyman asuycamuy	Come to my bosom;
Ccanmi canqui samillay	Thou art my joy.
Ñoccacc huahuay, hamuy, hamuy,	My child! Come! Come!
Cusiy cachun millay, millay,	My joy is many many times,
Chay sutitan churancayqui.	For I gave thee that name.
	[*Embraces her.*

YMA SUMAC.

Mamay! ymatan ruranqui	O mother! what do you do?
Ama ari saqque huaychu	Have I known thee only to weep?
Recsicuyqui llaquiypacchu	Hast thou left me alone?
Usucpacchu saqquehuanqui	To whom shall I fly?
Pimanatacc cutirisac	Where shall I turn?

Cutinipuyari ñahuiyman	To whom shall I turn my eyes?
Hampuy ari cay maquiyman.	Give me thy hands to help me.

PITU SALLA.

Ama ccapariychu ama	Do not weep,—do not
Ñoccapactac llaqui canman	For me ; it will be a torment.
Hacu puriy paccta uyaman	Let us go. March,
Mama cuna sapan cama.	The matrons may hear us.

YMA SUMAC.

Asllatahuan muchuriscay	Leave us a little longer
Cay aucca huatay huasita	In this hated prison.
Horccoscayquin qquepariscay	Let me stay here,
Cay pisi ppunchau ccasita	To pass a few days.
Ay Mama huañusccan rini	O mother, I go to death,
Munacuc sonccoypi miui.	And shall love poison for my heart. [*They shut the door.*

S C E N E   I I.

Enter CCAPAC YUPANQUI *and* UILLAC UMU.

CCAPAC YUPANQUI.

Hatun Auqui ! Uillac Umu !	Great Noble ! Uillac Umu !
Manachu canca yachanqui	Dost thou know ought
Ymatapas Rumimanta ?	Concerning Rumi-ñahui ?

UILLAC UMU.

Llocsinicañin hanacta	He went forth yesterday
Huillcañuta sacsacama	Towards Vilcañota.

Chaypin ricuni ascama	I see there
Huatasccata runacunata	Many men as prisoners,
Antipunin chaycunaca	All of them Antis.
Ñas atisca llapallancu	They are all conquered ;
Ñas ccosüiscan ahuarancu	Their homes are smoking ;
Ñas rupasccan tucuy ccacca.	Their fields are burnt.

CCAPAC YUPANQUI.

| Ollantayta happincuchus ? | Is Ollanta seized ? |
| Ycha quispin chay runacca ? | Is that man like straw ? |

UILLAC UMU.

| Chay rauraypin chay Ollantay | That Ollanta is taken, |
| Ñan raurascca llipillanta. | And conquered by the flames. |

CCAPAC YUPANQUI.

Yntin yanapahuasunchis	O Sun, thou hast favoured me,
Paypa yahuarñinmi cani	I am of thy blood.
Paycunatan ttustusunchis	They must submit to me,
Chaypacmi caypi sayani.	For this I stand here.

Enter a Messenger with a quipu, which he presents to the YNCA.

MESSENGER.

| Rumi-Ñahuin cachamuhuan | Rumi-Ñahui has sent me |
| Cay *quipu*huan ñacca paccar. | In quick haste, with this *quipu.* |

CCAPAC YUPANQUI.

| Ccan ricuy, ymatas ñin. | See thou, what it says. |

UILLAC UMU.

| Cay quipupin can quillinsa | In this *quipu* there is charcoal ; |

Ñan Ollantay rupasccaña	Then, Ollanta has been burnt.
Cay quiputacmi quimsa	Here there are three knots,
Pisca quipu huatasccaña	Fastened to five others ;
Ñan Anti-suyu happisca	That is, the Antis have sub-
Ñan Ynca maquiquipiñas	mitted,
	And are in the hands of the
Chaymi huatacun cay pisca	Ynca.
	Here are these three knots,
Yscay piscan tucuy piñas.	And two. All has been sternly
(*Quimsa*)	done.

CCAPAC YUPANQUI.

Ccancca chaypichu carccanqui	And thou, who wast there,
Ymatatacc rurarcanqui ?	What hast thou done ?

MESSENGER.

Ccapac Ynca! Ynti huahuay !	Great Ynca! child of the Sun
Caycca ñaupac apamuni	I have brought thee tidings,
Caycunata tactay chahuay	That thou hast triumphed—
Yahuarñinta upyaypuni	That their blood is shed.

CCAPAC YUPANQUI.

Cunancaiquichu manachu	Hast thou not been told,
Sayuntin runacunata	That the blood of these men,
Umapuni llocllancachu	Whom I pity and care for,
Runa yahuar paycunata	Is not to be shed ?
Cuyanim llaquinim ñispa?	That this would be a disaster ?

MESSENGER.

Manan Yaya hichaycuchu	O Father ! It is not done ;
Auccanchispa yahuarñinta	The blood of these traitors

Tutan happaycu llipinta	Is theirs still. This night
Callpan ashuan pupas puchu.	It might be taken.

CCAPAC YUPANQUI.

Ymatan can ricuncanqui?	What hast thou seen?

MESSENGER.

Chaypin ñoccapascarcani	I was there
Suyunchishuan cuscapuni	With all thy army—
Tinqui *Queru*pin puñuni	I was sleeping at the joining of the Queru—
Chaypitac pacacurcani	I was concealed
Suyuntin *Yanahuara*pi [65]	In the sides of Yana-huara.
Chaypin huayccu anchallatan	In that valley are many woods
Pacanapac chapran ccatan	In which to make an ambuscade.
Hinantinta chay huasipi	I was there in a house,
Quimsa ppunchau, quimsa tuta	For three days and nights,
Chay huayccupi pacacuni.	Concealed in that ravine;
Yarccaita chiri chucchuta [66]	There I felt cold and shivering.
Rumi-Nahuin hamun chayman	Rumi-Nahui came there
Hinapin llapata cunan	And told his plan:
Ccaya tutaman hamunqui	"You shall go at night,
Ñispa cutin sayananman	While I return to my place;
Hatun *Raymin* chay *tampupi*	In the Tambo they have a great *Raymi,*
Llapa llapan machacuncca	And all will be very drunk.
Hinaman llapa hamunca	Then come at night
Cozco-suyu tuta ucupi	With the army of Cuzco."
Chaypi ñispan cuticapun	So saying, he returned,

Noccaycuna sayascaycu	And we stood there
Chay tutata llapallaycu	All that night.
Hin ppunchau taripacun	That day was one of watching.
Ynti huatana ppunchaupi	As a day of gazing at the sun
Ollantacca ccochucuscca	Ollanta passed it
Payhuan cusca manchacuscca	And his men were drinking,
Hinantin runapas chaypi	And he with his men,
Ña quimsa ppunchau ticraspa	For a space of three days.
Chaupi tutan hatariycu	In the middle of the night,
Hahuanta mana rimaspa	Without any one speaking,
Tampumanmi yaycun llapa	We rushed into the *Tampu,*
Runayqui mana ccahuaspa	The men were not seen
Hinapin tarin toc llaspa	By those outside.
Llapata ccarac Yllapa [67]	It was like the lightning.
Tucuyñincun y manchascca	Fear fell upon them.
Hinata llipi llucuscca	They were caught in a net.
Hinatac ricchan huatascca	As they awoke, they were seized.
Ollantatan mascariyca	We sought for Ollanta ;
Ñan paytapas llucuscaña	He too was in the net.
Rumi-Ñahui y casccaña	Rumi-Ñahui was there ;
Uncu paypac hinan tariycu	We found him still sick.
Urco Huarancapas chaypin	There, too, was Urco Huaranca,
Ancha llaquisca qqueparin	Very sad at his condition,
Huascapi piñastan hapin	Chafing in his chains.
Hinan Ynca pusamunca	So the the Ynca guided
Ollantata suyuntinta	Ollanta with his followers.
Hanco-huaylluta huanmintinta	Hanco Huayllu with his women,
Llapa llantan atimuncu	All were conquered.
Chunca huaranca hinacha	Near a hundred thousand

G

Huatascca Antiquicuna	Antis were prisoners.
Ccatimumcun huarmicuna	The women followed near,
Huaccacuspa llaquipacha.	All of them weeping.

CCAPAC YUPANQUI.

Checantan can ricurcanqui	Truly thou hast seen
Uillcañuta putuyquipi.	Vilcañuta in mourning.

Drums, pipes, and flutes within.   Enter RUMI-ÑAHUI, *without his mantle.*

RUMI-ÑAHUI.

Huarancca cutin muchani	I worship a thousand times,
Ccapac Ynca, chaquiquita	Great Ynca! at thy feet.
Uyarihuay chay simita	Hear this mouth,
Maquiquipin pucarani.	My fate is in thy hands.

CCAPAC YUPANQUI.

Hatarimuy [ccani huarancca]	Rise! Take this my hand.
Cay maquiyman ancha cusi	This is thousandfold joy,
Ancha huichata cusi cusi	Joy above all joy for thee.
Chay unuta llicaptincca	Thou hast put a net in the water.
Llicampitac hapimunqui.	With thy net thou hast caught.

RUMI-ÑAHUI.

Rumihuanmi chay auccacca	If that traitor with his stones
Sipircan Auquicunata	Many noblemen has slain,
Chay millay runacunata	And thousands of others,
Rumitaccmi paypac ccacca	A rock and a stone to him
Ñoccan Rumi paypac cani	I, Rumi, have been,

Llapatañan huicupani.

And have made an end of all his people.

CCAPAC YUPANQUI.

Yahuarcca hichucurcanchu ?

Hast thou shed much blood ?

RUMI-ÑAHUI.

Manan Ynca mana puniu
    (*Auqui*)   (*punim*)
Hunttanin cunasccayquita
Huatamunin Antiquita
Orccon rauran, orccon rauran.
    (*tunin*)

No, Ynca, no, in truth,

Thy orders were obeyed—
The Antis are captured,
Their hills are burning.

CCAPAC YUPANQUI.

Maipitac chay auccacuna ?

Where are these enemies ?

RUMI-ÑAHUI.

Purunpin tucuy suyancu
Ccarac huc huañuyta sipipi
Ccoparispan llipi llipi
Huañunanta munascancu
Huarmincunan uma cama
    (*tucuy yoma*)
Huahuancupac ususcanmi
Tucuynincu huaccascanmi
Chaymi ttanichina cama.
(*Chaicanatan*)

All wait in the plain
To receive their deserts.
Each is awaiting
And desiring death.
But the women who are there,

And the little children,
Who are all weeping,
Must be separated.

CCAPAC YUPANQUI.

Hinan cancca hinapuni
Tucuy churin huaccha usurin
Tucuyñincun y ccolloncca

So let it surely be,
The poor and sick alike,
All must be left

Chayhuan Cuzcochin capuncca,

Chay auccacunata pusamuy!

To return to Cuzco.

Bring forth these traitors!

They bring forth OLLANTA, URCO HUARANCCA, *and*
ANCO-HUALLU.

Ñahuinta quichay chaycunata

Take off the bandages from
their eyes.

Ollantay maypin carcanqui?

Where art thou, Ollanta?

Maypin canqui Urco Huar-
ancca?

Where, Urco Huarancca, art
thou?

Cunanmi ticrasca canca.

Now thou art astonished.

They bring forth PIQUI CHAQUI *as a prisoner.*

Pitan horcco munqui chaypi?

Who is this brought with them?

PIQUI CHAQUI.

Chay yuncapin ancha piquin

Chaymi runata quirichan

Unu ccoñi chayta pichan

Chayllatan ñoccapacca sipui.

In the valleys are many fleas

That bite a man very sharp.

He is cured with hot water,

Therefore treat me the same.

CCAPAC YUPANQUI.

Anco-huallu, ñihuay ñihuay

Ymaraycan chincarcanqui?

Ymatan niy tanircanqui.

Ollantayhuan? rimanihuay.

Manachu Ynca yayaypas

Ccanta yupaycharccasurqui?

Manachuccan tarircanqui?

Paymanta yma haycatapas?

Anco-huallu, thou too here?

Why hast thou done this?

What canst thou say, for

Being with Ollanta? Speak.

Has not the Ynca, as a father,

Ever looked upon thee?

Hast thou not had thy desires?

What hast thou wanted?

Simiquin munayñin carccan	At thy word, thy wish was granted—
Ashuan mañacc ashuatacmi	And even more than thou hast asked.
Mañasccayquita hunttaccmi	When hast thou had a wish,
Ymatapas runacctacmi	What hast thou wanted
Ymatan ccampac pacarccan?	That has not been granted?
Rimariychis aucca-cuna	Speak, traitors!
Ollantay ñai! ñai Urco Huarancca.	Answer, Ollanta! And thou, Urco Huarancca.

OLLANTA.

| Ama tapuhuaychu Yaya | Father! We ask nothing ; |
| Huchaycun tucuypi phocchin. | Our sin is seen on all sides. |

CCAPAC YUPANQUI.

| Acllacuychis qquiriquita | Declare what they deserve. |
| Uillac Umu ccan rimariy. | Uillac Umu, speak thou. |

UILLAC UMU.

| Ñoccata ancha cuyactan | The sun has granted to me |
| Ynti sonccota ccohuarcan. | A very merciful heart. |

CCAPAC YUPANQUI.

| Rumi ccan ñatac rimariy. | Then speak thou, Rumi-Ñahui. |

RUMI-ÑAHUI.

Hatun huchaman chayayñincca	This being a great treason,
Quiri huañuypunin carccan	The punishment of these men
Chaymi runatacca harcan	Should be death,
Ashuan huchamanta Ynca.	For their crime against the Ynca.

Ttahua tacarpupi huatachun	They should be tied to four poles,
Sapa sapata cunallan	First one, and then another,
Hinatau tucuy llapallan	Until all are secured.
Huarmancuña y ttactachun	Then let all their servants
Tucuy huallahuisantapas	Pass over them.
Hinantin runa huachichun	Their men should be killed with arrows.
Yahuarñincupi macchichun	Thus in their blood shall we avenge
Yayancuc huañuscantari.	The deaths of our fathers.

PIQUI CHAQUI.

Hinanmanta chaymantari?	Would you do thus,
Tucuy Anti ppuchucachun	And destroy all the Antis?
(*Chhapracuñata rarachun*)	
Runata ruphananpaccri	Would you cut them to pieces?
[Uturuncu llana cachun.]	This is the work of a tiger.
	[*General lamentation within.*

RUMI-ÑAHUI.

Upallay runa!	Silence, man!
Rumitan checcocuscani	I am as a quarried stone,
(*huicapar*)	
Rumi sonccon cutiscani.	My heart is turned to stone.

CCAPAC YUPANQUI.

Uyarinquichischu ccancuna	Hast thou heard it?
Tacarpu camariscata	Thou shalt suffer at a stake.
Chayman pusay caycunata	Take them hence.

Anccataca sipiy chisña.   Death to the traitors!
(*Huanuchun cay auccacuna.*)

Rumi-Ñahui.

Aysay chayta huallahuisa   Drag them hence
Ccasonaman quinsantinta   To the place of execution.
Ricachun tucuy llipinta   Let them all be taken.
Ccasuscata : aysay! aysay!   Drag them away! Drag them
    away!

Ccapac Yupanqui.

Pascaychis chay huatascata   Unfasten those prisoners :
Hatarimuy cay ñauquiyman   Raise them from the ground.
Quespinquin huañuyniquita   Thou hast been near death.
    (*ricunqui sipeiquita*)
Cunan phahuay luychu[68] quita   Now fly like the deer.
Ñan urmanqui cay chaquiyman   Having fallen into my hands,
Cunanmi tecsi yachancca.   Thou shalt know thy fate.
Sonccoypi llampu cascanta   My heart is softened,
Hoccariscayquin y canta*   I will be generous to them,
Pachacutec chunca huarancca   Though their faults were ten
    thousandfold.

Canmi carcanqui huaminca   Thou who hast been hitherto
Anti-suyu camachicuc   The ruler of Anti-suyu,
Y ccantacmi cunan ricuy   Behold my resolution :
Ñoccac munaymiy captincca   I desire that thou continuest
Anti-suyuta camachiy   To rule in Anti-suyu,
Huaminccay capuy huiñaypac   That thy fame may last for ever.
Cay chucuta apay runaypac   Bring forth, for this man,

* These three lines are imperfect in Von Tschudi.

Campactacmi y cay huachay	The insignia of his rank.
Can Uillac Umu churapuy	Do thou, Uillac Umu, put them on ;
Mosocmauta [unan chata]	Let him wear them anew,
Hoccaripuay cay huacchata	Now his crime is removed,
Huañuscatari huacyapuy.	And he is freed from death.

UILLAC UMU.

Ollanta recsiyta yachay	Ollanta ! know now
Ccapac Yupanqui callpanta	The power of the great Yupanqui.
Payta ccatiy cunanmanta	Remember, from this day,
Cuyasccantari unanchay.	To learn thy duty.

Puts on OLLANTA *the helm, the golden bracelets, and gives him the arrows.*

Caypin callpa tucuy yachay	To obey his commands.
(*Cai sipipin tucuy callpai*)	
Chaytan cunan mattiycuyqui	Learn that these insignia
Cay champi Yncaccmi yachay.	Are the arms of the Ynca.

OLLANTA.

Hueqqueyhuanmi ccasparisacc	With tears I declare,
Cay cuyascayqui champita	That in receiving these arms,
Yanancani pachac mitta	I am a hundred times his servant.
Pitan can hinata tarisac !	Who shall equal me in this?
Cay sonccoytan chasqui chiqui	With this heart at thy feet,
Usutayquipi pumaypacc	I will unfasten thy shoe.
(*huatumpacc*)	

Cunanmanta huananaypacc   All my power depends
Tucuy callpaymi simiqui.   On the word of thy mouth.

Ccapac Yupanqui.

Urco Huaranca hamuy ccanri   Come here, Urco Huarancca!
Ollantan camarccasunqui   Ollanta promoted thee,
Huc chucuta ñoccamanri   But my anger is appeased.
Huc phiñayta chaytahuanpas   Thou shalt still continue
Ccanmi Antipi qqueparinqui   To command the Antis.
Canmi cunan puririnqui   Thou shalt march for me
Llullaycucc auccatahuanpas   To subdue my enemies.
Cay *chucu*tan cunnan ccoyqui   Receive this helmet,
Huaminccayñan ccampas can-   That thou mayst bear thyself
   qui   bravely.
Huañuymantan ccanta horccoy-   And now that thou art freed
   qui   from death,
Cuyascayta yupascanqui.   Thou art counted as one whom
    I love.

Urco Huarancca.

Millay cutin yupaychayqui   A thousand times art thou
    counted[n]

Ccapac Yupanqui ccantapas   For me, as the great Yupanqui,
Cay chucunta huachintapas   For bestowing this helmet.
(*Ccari-cay musucc tunqui*)
Muchaycuni Ñocca quitan   I adore thee humbly,
Llantayquiman haupullayqui.   And will be thy support.

Uillac Umu.

Huaminccantan rurasunqui   Thou art made noble

Ccapac Yupanqui ccantapas | By the great Yupanqui:
Cay chucunta huachintapas | With this helmet and these arrows,

Ccari cay ccan musucc tunqui. | Be valiant as the young *tunqui*.

RUMI-ÑAHUI.

Yscay ñachu ccanca Ynca | Then there will be two Yncas
Antisuyupi huamincca | In the warlike Anti-suyu.
[Puma pacchu cancca mirca | The lion will not brook
Yuncapi ancca matinca!] | An enemy in his valley.

CCAPAC YUPANQUI.

Manan Rumi yscaychu canca | No, Rumi; there will not be two.

Urco Huarancca camachincca | Urco Huarancca will rule
Anti-suyuta; chay captincca | In Anti-suyu.
Ollanta Cozcopi canca | Ollanta will in Cuzco
Yncarantin qqueparinan | Remain. For the Ynca,
Arpayñiypi [60] tiyaycuspa | He will occupy the throne,
Cozcota camachicuspa | And govern at Cuzco in his place.

Hinan caypi sayarinan. | Thus he will remain here.

OLLANTA.

Anchatan Yncay hoccarinqui | O Ynca! this is too much
Cay llatan yancca runata | For a man who is nothing.
Causacuy huarancca huata | Mayst thou live a thousand years.

[Chucchuctan cani achinqui | I am as thou makest me,
Ñoccatan hayhuaninchinqui | Thou dost give me succour:

Suchutan sayanichinqui	Crippled, thou makest me stand;
Urmacctan hattani chinqui	Fallen, thou raisest me up ;
Uscatan Ccapacyachinqui	Poor, thou enrichest me ;
Nausatan ccahuarichinqui	Blind, thou givest me sight ;
Huañuctan causanichinqui	Dead, thou restorest life ;—
Cconmactatac tac yachinqui].*	Thou indeed teachest me to forget.

[*Throws himself at the feet of the Ynca.*

CCAPAC YUPANQUI.

Hatun llaututa horccomuy	Place the yellow *llautu*
Qquellu umachata churaspa	On his head. Bring forth
Uillac Umu can utcaspa	The insignia, O Uillac Umu !
Hatum champitahuan ccomuy	Give him the great mace,
Ynca rantin cayca ñispa	That he may represent the Ynca,
Tucuyta cunan huillariy	And receive my orders.
Ccanri Ollanta qquepariy	Thou, Ollanta, wilt remain
Ynca ranti paccarispa	As Ynca in my place.
*Ccolla-suyu*manmi risac	I shall march to Colla-suyu
Cay quilla ucupi chaypacmi	In the space of a month,
Camarinay chay huantacmi	Therefore have I so ordered it.
(*chaypacctacmi*)	
Ashuan cusi puririsac	I shall go full of joy,
Ña arphaypi tiasccata	Leaving on the throne
Ollantata haqquecuspa.	My faithful Ollanta.

OLLANTA.

Ashuantan' munayman ccan-huan	I would rather desire

* This is omitted by Von Tschudi and Barranca.

Chayantaman tucuy imaman- pas	To march with thee.
Puriyta : yachanquim campas	Thou at least knowest
Cunchi cari cascay tahuan.	That I am diligent.
[Manan Cuzco huac yahuarchu]	My blood is not for Cuzco.
Cañariquin ñocca casac	I would be thy Cañari.°
Ñocapuni ñaupas casac	Surely I should be first
Ama caypi qquepaymanchu.	To march in thy company.

CCAPAC YUPANQUI.

Huarmita chasquiy ña ari	Be married in this place.
(*Huc cama casariy ari*)	
Chayhuan cusi camay canqui	With that thou shalt have joy,
Chayhuan ccasi samascanqui	And wilt rest in peace.
Pitapas acllacuy ari.	Choose whom thou wilt have.

OLLANTA.

Ñan auqui huarmiyoc cani	O my Lord ! I am married,
Nocca qquencha yanayquicca.	But I am also most miserable.

CCAPAC YUPANQUI.

Manatacmi ricsinichu	I have not yet seen
Ricsichihuay huarmiquita	Thy wife. Let me know her,
Yupaychasac yanayquita	I would count her as a friend.
Noccamanta pacahuanquichu.	Conceal nothing from me.

OLLANTA.

Cay Cozcopin chincarircan	In Cuzco I have lost
Chay huayllucuscay urpillaica	My most beloved turtle-dove.
Huc ppunchaullas pituy paicca	In a single day she was gone,
Huc pitaccmi phahuarinccan	Flying to other places.

Muspha musphan mascarcani	I have sought for her madly;
Hinantinta tapucuspa	But she is lost to me,
Allpa pumis millpupuspa	As if the earth had opened.
Chincachihuan : hinan cani !	Such is my misery !

CCAPAC YUPANQUI.

Ama Ollanta llaquicuychu	Do not despond, Ollanta !
Chaypas cachun y ymapas	Even were it worse,
Ccamascayta hunttay campas	Thou shouldest obey,
Ama qquepaman cutiychu	And not turn from thy duty.
Uillac Umu ñisccayta ruray.	Uillac Umu ! do as I ordered.

UILLAC UMU.

Hinantin suyu yachaychis	Know, all people,
Ollantaymi Yncacc rantim.	Ollanta is in place of the Ynca.

ALL.

Ollantaymi Ynca ranti.	Hail ! Ynca Ollanta.
	[*They all embrace each other.*

RUMI-ÑAHUI.

Cusuysiquin samiquita	I rejoice with thee,
Auqui Ollantay Ynca ranti.	Noble Ollanta ! Ynca !
Cusicuchun tucuy Anti	The Antis shall rejoice,
Hampuchuntac tucuy quita.	And all shall be well.

They seat OLLANTA *on a tiana, opposite to the* YNCA.

(*Voices within.*)

Harcay ! Harcay ! ccarcoy: ccarcoy :	Stop ! stop ! Turn her out !
Chay huarmata, ccarcoy.	Turn out that child !

YMA SUMAC (*within*).

[Cusi ppunchau casccan raycu]	Why should it be a day of joy?
Ashuan munasccayqui raycu	What dost thou love most?
Saqquehuachis yaycuycusac	Leave me to the father!
[Yncallahuan rimaycusac!]	Let me speak to the Ynca!
Amapuni harcahuaychu	Do not prevent me!
[Puncumanta ccarcu huaychu]	Let me pass the door!
Ricuy huañurcollasacmi	Lo! there is some one dying!
[Ricuychis sipicusacmi.] *	Lo! there is sickness, even to death!

CCAPAC YUPANQUI.

Yma chachuan huahuapi?	What are you doing with the child?

ATTENDANT.

Huc huarman huaccaspa hamun	A child comes weeping,
Yncahuan rimaytan munan.	And would speak with the Ynca.

CCAPAC YUPANQUI.

Haqquiy. Pusay camuy.	Let her come in.

Enter YMA SUMAC, *weeping, with her hair dishevelled.*

YMA SUMAC.

Mayquellanmi Yncallayca	Which of you is the Ynca,
Chaquinman ullpuycunaypacc?	That I may fall at his feet?

UILLAC UMU.

Caycca paymi Yncanchisca	That is our Ynca,
Ymananmi sumac huarma?	O beautiful child.

* The bracketed lines are omitted, both in Von Tschudi and Barranca.

/

YMA SUMAC.

Yncallay, Yayaymi canqui	My Ynca! thou art my Father!
Causachihuay huarmayquita!	Give life to thy child.
Hay huanihuay maquiquita	Show favour in thy hand,
Ynticcc huahuay ñinmi canqui	For thou art a child of the Sun.
Mamallaymi huañuccaña	My mother has been killed,
Huc aucca ccaccan mattiscan	An enemy has chained her.
Sulluncunapun sipiscan	She will be choked with streams
Yahuarñinpin ccaspascaña.	Flowing with her blood.

CCAPAC YUPANQUI.

Pin chay aucca utcay sacyariy	Who is this tyrant? Rise!
Ollantay ricuy ccan ari.	Ollanta! See thou to this.

OLLANTA.

Hacu, huarma, utccay pusahuay	Come, child, let us go.
Pin mamayquita sipiscan.	Who has hurt thy mother?

YMA SUMAC.

Amapuni ccancca riychu	Thou shalt not go,
Yncaypuni ricumuchun	The Ynca must see.
Paytac payta recsimuchun	He it is who knows her,
Manan ccanta resiquichu	While you do not.
Utccay Ynca sayarillay	Ynca, rise up quickly.
Paccta mamayta tariyman	Would you find my mother
Huañusccata y happinman	Lying dead? Listen,
Chalatanta: y uyarihuay.	And come to her.

UILLAC UMU.

Sapa Ynca manmi caman	Sole Ynca! Even thee
Llaquiscata mascasoncca	These miseries follow.
Ccampacca pitacc pacancca	Who shall dare
Quipichacta? hacu ccanhuan.	To shut thee out?

CCAPAC YUPANQUI.

Maypin quirin mamayquita?	Where is thy captive mother?

YMA SUMAC.

Cay cuchullapi, cay huasillapi.	In a corner in this house.

CCAPAC YUPANQUI.

Hacu ccatihuaypas huaquin	Let us all go together.
(*hacu llapa llapa*)	
Chica cusipi casccaptiy	When we were full of joy,
Cay huarma souccoyta ppaquin.	This child came to rend my heart.

YMA SUMAC *shows him the door of the prison.*

YMA SUMAC.

Caypin Yayay Mamallaycca	My Father! my mother
Caypipunin huañuñacha.	Is here. She may be dead.

OLLANTA.

Aclla huasitaccmi caycca	This is the house of the chosen virgins.
Ychachu pantanqui huarma?	Child, do you deceive us?

YMA SUMAC.

Cay huasipin urpillayca	In this house, my dove
Naccarin chunca huataña.	Has suffered for ten years.

OLLANTA.

Quichariy cay puncuta	Open this door,
Sapa Yncanchismi hamun.	The sole Ynca would enter.

Enter PITU SALLA, *who opens the door. All go in.*

YMA SUMAC.

Pitu Salla, ñañallay	Pitu Salla, my sister,
Causancacchu mamallayca ?	Is my mother yet alive ?
Hacu uccuman Yncallay	Enter with me, my Ynca,
Cay puncuta quicharichun.	Let the door be open.

SCENE III.

Enter YNCA YUPANQUI, UILLAC UMU, OLLANTA, YMA SUMAC, *and* PITU SALLA.

YNCA YUPANQUI.

Yma puncun caypi can ?	What door is this ?

YMA SUMAC.

Puncun caypi yayallay !	This is the door, my Father !
Pitu Salla, cay puncuta	Pitu Salla, open thou
Yncanchispac quicharipuy.	That door for our Ynca.

Enter CCACCA MAMA, *who kisses the* YNCA's *hand.*

CCACCA MAMA.

Mosccoypichu, suttinpichu ?	Is this but a dream ?
Yncayta caypi ricuni ?	Or do I see the Ynca here ?

H

Ynca Yupanqui.

Cay puncuta quichay.	Open that door.

(*The prison door is opened, and* Cusi Coyllur *is discovered senseless.*)

Yma Sumac.

Ay Mamallay! huattorcanmi	O my mother! my heart
Cay sonccoy camta tariyta	Told me
Huañusccata y nyayquita	That thou wert dead ;
Chintañan mancharccani	I feared to find it so.
Pitu Salla as unuta	Pitu Salla! bring me water,
Apamuy pacta mamay	Fetch it that my mother
Cutinpunman causiñinman.	May come back to life.

Ynca Yupanqui.

Yma utcu ccacan caycca?	What rock-hewn cave is this?
Pin cay huarmi yman chaccay	Who is this woman?
Quellay huasca huanquin chayta?	What means all this?
Pi auccan chacnarccan payta	What tyrant has thus chained her?
Maypin Yncac soncconpicca	Where was the heart of the Ynca?
Cay ccaraihuacca camasccan.	Has it produced some lizard?
Ccacca Mama hamuy canman	Come here, Ccacca Mama!
Pin cay hamun, caicca yman	What comes? Is it a rock?"
Layccasccachu paccarircan	Hast thou turned her to a ghost,
Cay huaccha huarmicca caypi?	That poor woman?

Ccacca Mama.

Yayayquin camachicurcan	Thy father ordered it,
Munaysapacc huananampac.	He willed it for her disobedience.

Ynca Yupanqui.

Llocsiy, llocsiy, Ccacca Maman,	Begone ! Begone ! Ccacca Mama,
Pusay chay uturuncuta	Turn out this jaguar,
Chay puma, chay amaruta,	This puma, this serpent ;
Ama haycacc ricunayman.	Never let me see her more.
[Ay qquechiychis chay auccata	Let that wretch escape,
Tunichiychis chay pirccata	Break down that wall,
Ticraychis rumi ccaccata	Turn over that stony rock,
Huicchuychis phunun auccata	Dismiss that traitress,
Mana ruracc mitccananman	Do not make her stumble.
Pinchay payata yuyanman	This is the secret place ;
Causac huarmi masinta	A woman living as a bat,
Sipiscascca huahuantinta.]	The child has brought it to light.

(They bring water and sprinkle it over Cusi Coyllur, *who comes to herself.)*

Cusi Coyllur.

Maypin cani, pin caycuna ?	Where am I ? who are these ?
Yma Sumac huahuallay	Yma Sumac ! my child !
Asuycamuy urpillay.	Come to me, my dove !
Hayccaccmantan runa cuna	Whence come these men ?
[Riccunimun cay ccayllaypi	Who are all these I see ?

Ricchay ñinchu ñahuillaypi?	What vision is before my eyes? •
Llautuchu runa ric chahuan	A man wearing the *llautu!*
Ycha phuyuchu quinpahuan?	What can it mean?
Ccanchaytanachu ricuni	I see lights darting ;
Causaymanchu cutinmuni.]	My life is overturned.

[*Begins to faint again.   Is restored with water.*

YMA SUMAC.

Ama Mamay manchariychu	Fear not, my mother,
Sapa Yncau cayman hamun	The sole Ynca has come to thee.
Ccapacc Yupanqui chayamun	The great Yupanqui is here.
Rimariy ama puñuychu.	Speak,—do not sleep.

YNCA YUPANQUI.

Sonccoymi ccasocun caña	My heart is torn
Cay llaquita ccahuarispa	At sight of such misery.
Ñihuay huarmi samarispa	Rest, woman. Then tell me
Pin canqui? Ñiy huc camaña	Who art thou? Say, child,
Yman sutin chay mamayquic?	What is the name of thy mother?

YMA SUMAC.   •

Huaccha-cuyac. Ccapac Ynca	Friend of the poor! great Ynca!
Chay huascataracc pascachiy	Order them to unchain her,
Cay huañusccata causachiy!	Give life to the dead.

UILLAC UMU.

Ñoccan chaytacca pascanay   I ought to free her,
Ñaccaricta yanapanay.   I should be her friend.

OLLANTA.

Yma sutin mamayquicca?   What is the name of thy
                           mother?

YMA SUMAC.

Cusi Ccoyllur sutincca.   Cusi Coyllur is her name.

YNCA YUPANQUI.

Ñan ricunqui pantasccatu   You seem to be mistaken in
Chay sutinta, pampasccata   That name.   She is gone
Maypis capunpas samincca.   Where she has happiness.

OLLANTA.

Ay Ccapac Ynca Yupanqui   O great Ynca Yupanqui,
Cay Ñustan ñocca chuarmiycca. That Princess is my wife.

[Prostrates himself at the feet of the YNCA.

YNCA YUPANQUI.

Mosccoymanmi ricchapuan   It all seems a dream,
Cay tariscusccay samiycca   This newly found joy,
Cay Cusi Ccoyllur huarmiycca   This woman is Cusi Coyllur!
Pañaymi hina capuan   Here at my right hand,
Cusi Ccoyllur panallay   Cusi Coyllur, my sister!
Cusi Ccoyllur urpillay   Cusi Coyllur, my dove!
Hampuy cutimpuy   Come here, and embrace me.
[Ric nayquipi chasquipuay   See now thou art delivered,

Turayquin taricapuyqui]	Thou hast found thy brother,
Ccasccoymi cascan chimpayqui	My bosom will be thy home,
[Tcccsinpi tianayquipacc.]	Thy resting-place shall be se-
	cure,
Cusiña causanayquipac.	Thy life shall be joyful.

[Embraces her, and seats her by his side.

CUSI COYLLUR.

Ay turallay ! ñas yachanqui	Oh my brother! now thou
	knowest
Hayccan ñaccanicusccayta	The torments I suffered
(*Cai chica*)	
Ascca huanusccayta	For so many years.
(*Chica huata ñaccariscatta*)	
Ccan puritacc cunan canqui	Thou hast set me free ;
(*Campunin canqui*)	
Cay piñasta quespichicca	It is thou that hast loosened
(*quirita*)	me,
[Cay ppanpascca haspichicca.]	Thou hast dug me out.

YNCA YUPANQUI.

Pin cay cullcu chic puticc	Who art thou, dove, that hast
(*huarmi*)	suffered ?
Pin cayman churarccan cayta	Who placed thee here ?
Yma huchan payta aysayta	What sin had weighed thee
	down ?
Atiparccan cayman uticc ?	Well mightest thou have gone
	mad.
Canchu soncco ccahuanapac	I should have a heart to feel
Cay chica sinchi llaquita	Such dreadful suffering.

Picha huacharccan cay huarmita
Payhuan cusca huañunapacc
Chay uyan ccampamanasca
Chay sumac simi phasquiscca
[Uya ccaccllan yanccayascca
Senccallampas chiri asccu
Ric chayñillanpas ayacc na
Cuncallapas chaca raccna.

If this woman was thy mother
Yet she ought to die.
Thy face is withered,
Thy beauty is gone for ever,
Thy chin is turned black,
Thy nose is like a cold potato,
Thy looks are as death,
Thy neck is withered.

OLLANTA.

Cusi Ccoyllur y ccantaracc
Chincachircayqui ñaupacta
Cunantac ñocca causaccta
    (*canri*)
Yayahuanqui sipiytaracc
Yscayñinchisña huañusun
Huanullasac sapay huaychu
(*Ama qqueparichin huaychu*)
Cay sonccoymi sapan usun
Cusi Ccoyllur maytacc cusi?
Maytacc chay Ccoyllur ñahuy-
    qui?
Maypitacc chay samayñiqui
Ccanchu chay ñacascca ususi?

Cusi Coyllur, I lost thee,
Thou wast first hidden from me,
But now thou art brought to
    life,
And thy father could do this!
He should have killed us both!
I would not be left alone,

My whole heart is torn.
Cusi Coyllur, where is thy joy?
Where are thine eyes like stars?

Where is all thy beauty?
Art thou an accursed daughter?

CUSI COYLLUR.

Ay Ollantay, chunca huatan
Caracc miyu raquihuanchis
Cunautacc huñupuhuanchis

Alas! Ollanta, for ten years
A prison has separated us;
But now we are joined again,

Huc causayman : hinan huatan	And there is life ! As many years
Llaqui cusita Yupanqui	Of joy you will count
Causachuntacc Ccapac Ynca	As the great Ynca shall live.
Ccanri huc causay cactincca	With this new life
Ascan huatatan Yupanqui.	You will count more years.

UILLAC UMA.

Musuc ppachata apamuy	Bring new clothes
Ñustanchista pachanapac.	To dress the princess.

[They all begin to embrace each other.

. YNCA YUPANQUI.

Ollantay caycca huarmiyqui	Ollanta, here is thy wife,
[Caytaccmi chay ususiyqui	Here, too, is thy daughter,
Hunucuychis musucmanta]	In a new union ;
Yupay chacuy cunanmanta	Count it so, from this day.
Ccanri hamuy, Yma Sumac	And thou, Yma Sumac, come to me—
Cay ccasccoyman sumac urpi	Come here, my beautiful dove,
Huanquicuscay cay cururpi	Thou must reel these threads,
Ccanmi canqui Ccoyllur chuma.	Since thou art the child of Coyllur.

OLLANTA.

Ccanmi canqui achihuaycu	Thou art our protection !
Ccan auqui maquiquiman	Thy noble hands
Tucuy phuti ñanta pantan	Disperse our grief ;
Ccan llapata saminchahuaycu.	Thou art our only hope.

YNCA YUPANQUI.

Chicallata phuticuychis	Do not be afflicted,
Samaniychisña samipi	Live happily with thy joy ;
(*Cusi cachun huc samipi*)	
Ñan huarmiyqui maquiquipi	Now thy wife is in thy hand,
Cusillaña causa aychis.	And thy life is full of joy.
(*Huañuimantan qquespinqui-*	
chis.)	

(*They play huancars,*[70] *pincullus,*[71] *purutus,*[72] *and other music.*)

NOTES.

—◇—

(1) *Pachacutec.* The ninth Ynca, according to Garcilasso de la Vega. The meaning of the word is, "The earth overturned." *Pacha* (earth), *Cutini* (I overturn). So called from his having been a great reformer.

(2) *Yupanqui,* son of Pachacutec, and tenth Ynca. It was a title of all the Yncas. Literally "You will count," 2d person singular of the indicative future, from *Yupani* (I count). He who bears the title *will count* as one who is excellent in virtue and piety. (*G. de la Vega,* I. lib. ii. cap. 17.)

(3) The name does not occur elsewhere, and has no meaning. But see note in Introduction, p. 11.

(4) *Rumi* (a stone) and *ñahui* (eye). The name occurs again, as that of a general of Atahuallpa.

(5) *Uillac Umu,* the title of the High Priest. *Uillac* is the past participle of *Uillani* (I say), and *Umu* (a diviner). He was the diviner who *said* to the people what the Sun ordained. (*G. de la Vega,* III. cap. 22.)

(6) *Urco* (a male) *Huarancca* (a thousand).

(7) *Hancu* (raw) *Huayllu* (love), *Auqui,* a nobleman, an unmarried prince. There was a famous rebel chief of the Chancas named Hancohualla, but this does not appear to be the same word.

(8) *Piqui* (a flea) *Chaqui* (foot).

(9) *Ana Huarqui.* The sister and wife of the Ynca Pachacutec. See *G. de la Vega*, II. p. 203.

(10) *Cusi* (joyful) *Coyllur* (star).

(11) *Yma* (how) *Sumac* (beautiful).

(12) *Ccacca* (rock) *Mama* (mother).

(13) *Pitu* (equal) *Salla* (rocky ground).

(14) A genitive form, common in early Quichua writing, for Yncap. *cc* or *cca* as genitives, in place of *p* and *pa*, often occur in this drama.

(15) *Urpi* (a dove) : a term of endearment.

(16) *Raicuni*, I invite, mislead, bewitch.

(17) *Musphani*, I wander, am puzzled.

(18) This is the perfect optative. Von Tschudi criticises the passage and thinks that *sipiyquiman* would have been better.

(19) *Allco* is the Peruvian dog (*Canis Ingæ. Tsch.*) It has been found buried at the feet of mummies.

(20) I gave an erroneous translation of this passage in my *Cuzco and Lima*, p. 174, which was furnished to me by a young student of Cuzco. The blunder is noted by Señor Barranca, p. 56.

(21) *Ccepi* is a burden or load, and it is here used figuratively by Piqui Chaqui for a porter or menial.

(22) *Laicca*, a soothsayer or wizard. See *G. de la Vega* and *Arriaga*.

(23) *Cachapuriy*, your messenger. Garcilasso has *Chaca*, and *Chasqui*. See *G. de la Vega*, II. p. 119.

(24) Von Tschudi and Barranca have *Huillca uma* in their copies ; and Von Tschudi, in a note, says that *Uillca uma* would be better. Barranca gives a derivation from *Huillca,* "grandfather," and *uma,* "head." But my copy has *Uillac Umu,* the correct term for the High Priest of the Sun. Garcilasso derives it from *Uillani* (I say), and *Umu,* a diviner or soothsayer. *Uillac* is the present participle, and the meaning of *Uillac Umu* is " The diviner who speaks." Garcilasso has V for U. (*G. de la Vega,* I. p. 227.)

(25) *Rupicola Peruviana (Dum),* a beautiful bird with a rich orange plumage and a tuft, used with other birds in sacrifices.

(26) *Llautu,* the crimson fringe of the Ynca, equivalent to saying that the Ynca will share the throne with him.

(27) *Toclla,* a lasso. *Tocllani,* I catch with a lasso.

(28) The copies of Von Tschudi and Barranca have *Quellca,* "to write," a word of doubtful antiquity. In my copy the ancient word *quipu* is used.

(29) *Hatun Yaya,* Great Father, a term applied to the High Priest.

(30) *Atoc,* the Peruvian fox. Von Tschudi's copy has *Asnu* (from the Spanish for an ass), and Barranca's *Llama.* Barranca points out that *asnu* is the insertion of a careless modern copyist. I believe *llama* to be a correction hazarded by Señor Barranca. *Atoc* alone suits the text ; and is, no doubt, the most ancient reading.

(31) *Rirpu* is a mirror, made of polished metal. This speech of Cusi Coyllur is given in the *Antiguedades Peruanas,* p. 117.

(32) In my copy it is *Accochinchay,* a comet. In those of Von Tschudi and Barranca the word is *Chasca,* the planet Venus.

(33) Here Von Tschudi's copy is faulty. He has *chaquirichci.* It should be *chaquichicuy* (dry again).

(34) The *Tuya* is a bird that is very mischievous at harvest time (*Coccoborus chrysogaster*). *lla* is a diminutive, and *y* is the first possessive pronoun.

(35) Barranca tells us that eleven species of Peruvian doves have been described, four by Von Tschudi. *Urpi* is the general name for a dove.

(36) *Yarahui*, an elegy.

(37) The ending *chis*, which often occurs in the drama, is an ancient form.

(38) Huanca Uillca was a great chief of the Chancas, who rebelled against the Yncas.

(39 *a*) Here the particle *ñi* is inserted for euphony.

(39 *b*) This speech of Ollanta is given in the *Antiguedades Peruanas*, p. 117, but without any translation.

(40) The *Antis* were the inhabitants of the region east of Cuzco.

(41) *Sacsahuaman* was the hill on which the famous fortress of Cuzco was built.

(42) Here Von Tschudi has *misi*, a modern word for a cat, instead of *allco*, as in my copy. See *G. de la Vega*, II. p. 476.

(43) The doors were fastened by a rope, called *huascar*.

(44) *Achancaray*, a red and white flower with which the Indians adorn their hair; a begonia.

(45) *Lloclla*, a flood or torrent. In the country of Chincha-suyu the word for a torrent is *Thuancu*, and in the Mochica language, on the coast, it is *Yapana*.

(46) *Urubamba* is a pleasant town near Cuzco, in the valley of the Vilca-mayu.

(47) *Yacollo*, a mantle.

(48) *Puna-runa. Puna*, the lofty and thinly inhabited regions of the

Andes. *Runa*, a man. It seems to imply that the inhabitants of the *Punas* were timid.

(49) *Llullu ccachu.* Literally a feeble herb, scarcely raising its head above the ground. The word *ccachu* belongs to the dialect of the Collas.

(50) *Miu* is poison.

(51) *Queru*, a mountain stream, flowing into the Vilca-mayu.

(52) *Pachar* is a ravine near Ollanta-tambo, opening on to the Vilca-mayu valley.

• (53) *Aclla*, chosen. "The chosen ones," as the Virgins of the Sun were called.

(54) *Taparacu* is a large butterfly; the appearance of which inside a room was looked upon as a bad omen.

(55) *i.e.*, surrounded by dangers.

(56) The birds used for sacrifice were the *Tunqui* (*Rupicola Peruviana*), the *Cuntur*, and the *Parihuana* or flamingo.

(57) *Rumi-tunqui* is a play on the name of the general.

(58) Barranca compares this strategy of Rumi-Ñahui to that of Zopyrus, as described by Herodotus.

(59) Here Rumi-Ñahui is again punning on his name of *a stone.*

(60) *Nucchu*, the Salvia. *Sunchu* is a large yellow *composita*. The Indians used to boil the leaves, dry them in the sun, and keep them to eat in winter (*G. de la Vega,* II. p. 376.) The exact meaning of the passage is obscure.

(61) For an account of the celebration of the Raymi, see *G. de la Vega*, II. p. 22, 155, 162, 445. *Ynti-huatana* was a circle of stones whence the sun was observed by the priests and people. *Ynti* is the sun. *Huatana* is from *Huatani* (I seize.) (*G. de la Vega*, I. p. 177.) Hence *Huatana*, a lasso or halter; and hence a circle, and *Huata* a year. (*G. de la Vega*, I. p. 177.)

(62) *Siclla*, a blue flower.

(63) *Chayña*, a little singing bird (*Chrysomitris Magellanica*).

(64) *Panti*, a bush with a beautiful purple flower (*Lasiandra Fontanesiana*).

(65) *Yanahuara*, a ravine opening on the valley of the Vilca-mayu between Urubamba and Ollanta-tambo.

(66) *Chucchu* is the cold fit, in an ague. Hence shivering.

(67) *Ccarac yllapa*, thunder and lightning, all the accompaniments of a thunderstorm.

(68) *Luychu* (*Cervus Antisiensis, D'Orb.*)

(69) This is obscure. *Arpay* means a blood sacrifice. Barranca says that it also signifies a throne of gold, synonymous with *tiana*.

(70) *Huancar*, a drum.

(71) *Pincullu*, a flute.

(72) *Purutu*, a bean. Some sort of rattle.

———

(a) *Dances of straw.* The ancient Peruvians hung fertile stalks of maize, called *huantay-sara* and *arihuay-sara*, on the branches of trees, and danced the *arihuay* or harvest dance under them. The stalks were afterwards burnt as a sacrifice to the thunder god. See *Extirpacion de la idolatria de los Indios del Peru. Pedro de Arriaga*, 1621.

(b) The *Raymi* was the chief festival of the Sun. For a full account of the ceremonies connected with it, see *G. de la Vega*, II. p. 155.

(c) *Rupicola*, a bird from the warm forests, with bright orange plumage and tuft.

(d) *Situa Raymi* was the fourth annual feast in honour of the Sun. See *G. de la Vega*, II. p. 228.

(e) *Auqui* is the title of an unmarried prince. In the dialects of the Collas, as well as in those of Chinchay-suyu, this word is used for father.

(*f*) A district to the south of Lake Titicaca.

(*g*) *Rumi-Ñahui* is represented as the general or leader of *Hanan-Suyu* or the upper district, which I take to mean *Hanan* (or upper) Cuzco.

(*h*) Natives of the coast valleys.

(*i*) The Chancas inhabited the country between Cuzco and Guamanga. They were utterly defeated and conquered by Uira-ccocha, the father of Pachacutec, but not before their formidable insurrection had shaken the Ynca power to its foundations.

(*j*) The heroic chief of the Chancas, defeated in the time of the Ynca Uira-ccocha.

(*k*) *Macana* is a war club.

(*l*) This is a pun of Piqui Chaqui. Huarancca means a thousand, but it is also the name of Ollanta's chief lieutenant.

(*m*) *Uillcañuta* is the snowy peak in sight from Cuzco (*G. de la Vega*, II. p. 255). Ollanta, as the highest of men, is compared to the loftiest among peaks. *Uillca* means anything sacred.

(*n*) The use of the word *count* in these passages, is intended as a pun on the name of the Ynca *Yupanqui* ("You will count"). See note (2.)

(*o*) "*I would be thy Cañari.*" This line fixes the date of the play, as in the reign of the Ynca Huayna Ccapac, who died in 1525; or, at the earliest, in that of his father Tupac Yupanqui, who conquered the province of the Cañaris (*G. de la Vega*, II. p. 335). The Cañaris were famous for their loyalty as vassals of the Yncas; and hence the word *Cañari* became synonymous for a loyal subject (*G. de la Vega*, II. p. 336 *and note*). Afterwards their character changed, and they traitorously helped the Spanish invaders, and betrayed their old masters on all occasions.

(*p*) "*Is it a rock?*" This is a play on the name of Mama Ccacca, a woman as relentless and hard as a rock. *Cacca* means a rock in Quichua; while *Caca* is an uncle, being brother of the mother.